CUMULUS CONGESTUS OR MEDIOCRIS

CUMULONIMBUS CALVUS

CUMULON CAPILL

OF LUS DUS

CIRRUS FIBRATUS

CIRRUS SPISSATUS

CIRRUS SPISSATUS CUMULONIMBOGENITUS

CIRRUS FIBRATUS OR UNCINUS

CIRRUS & CIRROSTRATUS

CIRRUS & CIRROSTRATUS

ALTOSTRATUS TRANSLUCIDUS

CUMULUS HUMILIS OR FRACTUS

MARCIA WILLIAMS

CLOUD BOY

PATCHES OF ALTOCUMULUS TRANSLUCIDUS

ALTOCUMULUS CASTELLANUS OR FLOCCUS

CIRRUS & CIRROSTRATUS

CIRROCUMULUS

STRATOCUMULUS CUMULOGENITUS

CUMULUS HUMILIS OR FRACTUS

WALKER BOOKS

CUMULUS & STRATOCUMULUS

CUMULUS CONGESTUS OR MEDIOCRIS

ALTOCUMULUS CASTELLANUS OR FLOCCUS

ALTOSTRATUS TRANSLUCIDUS

NIMBOSTRATUS OR ALTOSTRATUS OPACUS

STRATOCUMULUS NON-CUMULOGENITUS

STRATOCUMULUS CUMULOGENITUS

ALTOCUMULUS TRANSLUCIDUS

PATCHES OF ALTOCUMULUS TRANSLUCIDUS

ALTOCUMULUS TRANSLUCIDUS (IN BANDS)

ALTOCUMULUS OPACUS OR DUPLICATUS

ALTOCUMULUS CUMULOGENITUS

CIRRUS FIBRATUS OR UNCINUS

CIRRUS & CIRROSTRATUS

CIRRUS & CIRROSTRATUS

CIRROSTRATUS

CIRROSTRATUS

For Olga – with love and thanks

First published 2019 by Walker Books Ltd, 87 Vauxhall Walk, London SE11 5HJ

2 4 6 8 10 9 7 5 3

This book has been typeset in Caslon Book, Ashley Script and QuicksansAccurate

Printed and bound in Great Britain by CPI Group (UK) Ltd, Croydon, CR0 4YY

British Library Cataloguing in Publication Data: a catalogue record
for this book is available from the British Library

ISBN 978-1-4063-8121-4

www.walker.co.uk

THIS DIARY BELONGS TO:

ANGELA MOON
32 ORCHARD ROAD,
LONDON, ENGLAND.

MY FAMILY

MUM: *Gilly Moon*

DAD: *Mickie Moon*

BABY BROTHER: *Solo Moon*

GRANNY: *Joan ~ always travelling, hardly ever seen*

GRANDMA: *Gertrude ~ really my GREAT-grandma. WARNING: Do not mention the "great", she likes to ignore her superior age!*

PET: *Edith the goldfish ~ almost dead!*

MY HOBBIES: *Art, art and art!*

BEST BOOK: *Sketch book*

BEST FRIEND: *Harry Christmas*

HARRY'S FAMILY

HARRY'S MUM: *Lilly Christmas*

HARRY'S DAD: *Joe Christmas*

SIBLING: *Due November, sex unknown*

GRANNY: *No grandparents, only unmentionable cousins*

PET: *Dog pending ... (in his dreams!)*

HARRY'S HOBBIES: *Cloud spotting and cloud talking! Harry has taught me loads about cloud types and their symbols — he's a cloud nerd!*

BEST BOOK: The Cloud Book

BEST FRIEND: *Me, Angie Moon!*

MAY

MY FAVOURITE MONTH

8TH MAY, MY BIRTHDAY!

CLOUDS: *Not a cloud in the sky — bad luck, Harry, you cloud freak!*

Dear Diary,

I may as well tell you straight away that I hate writing! Every year someone gives me a diary for my birthday and every year I give up after a couple of pages. Just because I am another year older doesn't mean that I'm suddenly going to turn into a writing sort of person. I will try, but I don't promise.

Anyway, I did have an awe-inspiring birthday. I always share my party with Harry, my neighbour and best friend. Our mums had us in the same hospital just two days apart, so we are almost-twins. I'm the oldest though, and I won't let Harry forget it! We used to hold hands whenever we were together but that was when we were little – now we just call each other rude names. They're the same names we used as little kids. Mine for him is "hedgehog" because he's always had a prickly nature. His for me is almost too embarrassing to write, but I will – it's "knickers". When we were tiny we thought it was a rude word and it sent us into fits of giggles. Somehow it's just stuck, but I wish it hadn't. Both names are strictly between us. We think we might get married one day, but we're not sure about having kids!

For our birthday present Dad and Joe, who is Harry's dad, are going to build a tree house spanning our two gardens, which will be truly awesome! They are going to put windows in the roof so that Harry can spot the clouds and

I can paint them. Harry is a cloud collector, which means you keep a note of every crazy cloud you see, with names, dates, shapes and weather fronts. I'm a cloud artist, which means I do endless pictures of clouds – mostly in animal shapes. Harry wanted a puppy for his birthday as well as the tree house, but his mum is having a baby so that's not going to happen.

After all our party guests had gone home, Harry and I did a celebration bounce on my bed. Bouncing used to be our best thing. We've been doing it since for ever – only we're definitely too big now and are in danger of breaking the bed. You should have heard the creaks. Unfortunately, Harry had eaten too much birthday cake and was sick – a gross vomiting hedgehog on my best new bedcover!

13TH MAY, THE GRAND ORCHARD ROAD BUILD

CLOUDS: *Cirrus castellanus*

MORNING

Dear Diary,

Are you amazed that I'm still here? I am! This is my second day of writing – I must have turned over a new leaf.

Our dads can be the most annoying people in the whole wide world! Me, Harry and the two dads went to buy wood and stuff for the tree house. Well, that was the plan, but first the dads had to have a coffee and then we had to go and buy nappies for Solo, my puking and pooing baby brother. When we finally got to the wood place it was lunch time and Harry had a hunger headache and my tummy was rumbling, so we had to be really quick. As a result we've accidentally bought enough wood for a tower block.

AFTERNOON

Dad and Joe are in the garden building our tree house. Mum says there's a load more chat than action, but I'm really excited and so is Harry. He says the clouds are very auspicious. They are cirrus castellanus, which are cirrus clouds with turrets and battlements, so we think we might end up with a castle, which would be even better than a tower block! Harry and I tried to help, but the dads shouted at us for getting in the way. We'd like to know whose tree house this is – wouldn't we Harry?

Yes, we damn well would! – H

Harry and I watched the grand Orchard Road build from my bedroom for a while, but that was boring. Instead we decided to get our own back on the dads for shouting at us. We got our magnifying glasses and hunted for dead insects. We found one spider, two flies, one buggy thing and half a worm.

We ground them all into flour and added them to some bun mixture. Then we baked them, iced them and served the buns to the dads with a cup of tea. They ate them with relish! Well, as Mum would say, they were full of protein. We waited for the dads to be sick, but they weren't – shame. I bet they would have been if we'd told them what they'd eaten, but we didn't dare.

What Angie means is that she didn't dare!
Yours, Harry.

19TH MAY,
DOWN WITH HEDGEHOGS!

CLOUDS: *Cumulus congestus*

Diary,

I am not happy and neither are the clouds. Harry says they often reflect his mood and today they certainly reflect mine. Cumulus congestus clouds can cause short, sharp downpours and I am about to pour down my short, sharp anger!

Harry has not been at school all week and I know he's just pretending to be ill. He doesn't want to be in the school play and I can't blame him. He is always the lead because he's got cute blond curls and can sing, but he says that having to learn all the lines makes his head ache. Still, that is no reason to leave me struggling with our rubbish teacher, Miss Lemonpops, or the grungy girls in the class who hate me.

I went round to see Harry after school,

but his mum said he was in bed. I doubt that. Anyway, she looked as though she'd been crying so I didn't push it. I told her that I'd call round in the morning to see how Harry is. Mum says pregnant women cry all the time and boys love their beds!

Dad came home early and we worked on the tree house together. It is going to be awesome. Today we built a ladder so that we can access it safely – at least from my side. That Harry Hedgehog person might just have to stay on the ground, looking up at me and wishing.

20TH MAY,
A CREPUSCULAR DAY

CLOUDS: *Cumulus humilis —*
white cotton puffs with flat bases

Hello Diary,

I just want to say that I don't know why I'm noting the clouds – Harry's the cloud collector, not me. He has books and books of notes on the things. Really I just like drawing clouds and looking for animal shapes in them, especially dog and horse shapes. Cumulus clouds make the best animal shapes and if you are very lucky, and the sun is shining behind them, they can be lit up around the edges by "crepuscular rays". Anyway, it has been a truly monumental, "crepuscular ray" day because the tree house is nearly finished. Talk about dad power! One minute it was all chat and no action, and the next minute there it is ... almost. And, wow, it is crazy wonderful!

Harry appears to be better, probably because

there is no school, so we are having a sleepover tonight. In fact, right now this minute! Tomorrow we are going to complete the last of the building work and start decorating the tree house. Aren't we Harry? He's asleep – the hibernating hedgehog. I'll have to wake him later for our midnight feast: crisps, jelly babies, iced buns (without bugs), cold sausages and cucumber sticks (Mum's health-conscious contribution!).

21ST MAY, ARTCLOUD

CLOUDS: *None, but lots of contrails from aeroplanes*

I won't keep drawing attention to this as it might get a bit boring, but do you realise that today is my FIFTH day of writing?! Well, if you're not impressed now, dear Diary, you will be when you hear my news.

The tree house is finished and – you are not going to believe this – it has lights! There's a pulley with a basket on the end so we can haul stuff up and down. There are now two ladders so that you can access it from Harry's garden or mine, a walkway and a little, low door leading into one big room. All the windows are in the roof, but the walls have spyholes in them so we can see out but no one can see in – isn't that the best idea!

The decorating isn't finished yet, but the building absolutely is. We all had supper up there, even Solo. It was a bit of a squash, but fantastically brilliant. We put down a rug and sat on cushions so it was like a posh picnic. We had fizzy drinks and a naming ceremony.

"I name this tree house Artcloud, and may all who sway in her keep safe!"

We thought of the name together, art for me and cloud for Harry – cool or what?! When it gets a bit warmer we are going to sleep in Artcloud every night. I think I could live there for ever and ever!

P.S. We are going to paint the walkway blue and white, so it looks as though we have a house floating on a cloud.

P.P.S. Harry was sick this morning. I suspect too many cold sausages. Or maybe it was the cucumber sticks – it never pays to be too healthy!

27TH MAY,
HOORAY FOR HALF TERM!

CLOUDS: *Beautiful, beautiful clouds in wild shapes*

Dearest and most lovely Diary,

Half term starts here! The sun is shining and we are moving in to Artcloud. Harry and I intend to spend the whole day up here cloud spotting, drawing, nibbling and nesting. We have pooled all our pocket money and bought an old ship's bell, which Dad is going to help us fix by the door. Then we can call each other whenever we want.

One ring: "I'm here if you want to join me."

Two rings: "I'm here with food to share!"

Three rings: "Come quick, I need you urgently!"

I would just like to point out that I put in more money than Angie, so only the gong bit is hers and the rest of the bell is mine. Yours, Harry.

Well, Harry Christmas, I'd just like to point out that the message is the same whoever flipping paid for it!

Ignore that, Diary, because I have another piece of important news: tomorrow Grandma Gertie, star name Gertrude Olive Moon, is coming to stay! I can't tell you why she's a star right now as I've got to help Harry and Dad fix the bell, but all will be revealed tomorrow!

28TH MAY, INTRODUCING MY GRANDMA GERTIE

CLOUDS: *Altostratus opacus —*
grey, dull and annoying

Dear Diary,

No Artcloud this morning, instead we are all going to the grand opening of a quilt exhibition. That may sound really, really boring but actually it's pretty cool and even Harry wants to come. One of the exhibits is a quilt that my Grandma Gertie helped to make when she was a child prisoner during World War Two.

When Grandma was a bit younger than me she lived in Singapore, with her little brother Peter and their dad and mum. Singapore was a British military base and her dad worked there as an engineer, but two years after the outbreak of the war, Singapore was invaded by Japan. Japanese soldiers rounded up all the British and Australian families and imprisoned them, mostly in Changi Prison. I don't know a lot about it, but I do know that Grandma and some of the other children in the prison made a patchwork quilt for their Girl Guide leader. It must be quite special because Grandma's been talking about it on the radio and on the telly. Grandma was the youngest child working on the quilt and she is over 80 now, so I think that she might be the only one of them still alive.

LATER

Just back from the exhibition and it turns out that my grandma really is a star – well she kept that very quiet! The Changi quilt was quite small and faded, but everyone at the museum thought it was extremely special. You could still see some of the girls' initials in the middle of their patchwork rosettes – Grandma's was the best, of course. Each rosette was made of different scraps of dress cotton; Grandma said she could remember where every bit of fabric had come from and that it brought her memories of Changi flooding back.

Harry wanted to hear all about the jail and what it was like to be a prisoner, but I don't think Grandma wanted to talk about it – it probably made her too sad. There were photos of the prison beside the quilt and it looked truly terrible – the poor prisoners were stick-thin and almost naked. Grandma said that was because their clothes had rotted away in the sun. I don't know how those children stayed alive, let alone thought of making someone a beautiful quilt.

I'm so happy Grandma is staying with us, because I wouldn't want her to go home and be full of sad memories. Since Grandpa Jimmy died, Grandma likes to stay at her house among his things, but as Solo has totally given up sleeping, and Mum is completely exhausted, Grandma said she'd stay to help out for a while. This is an excellent idea as Solo is permanently attached to Mum and she often forgets that I exist. I hope Grandma stays for a looooooooooooooooooooong, loooooooooooong time!

I bought this postcard of Grandma Gertie's

quilt for my diary – it's funny, but I think it looks just like Grandma, even though she only sewed one little rosette (an arrow marks the spot!).

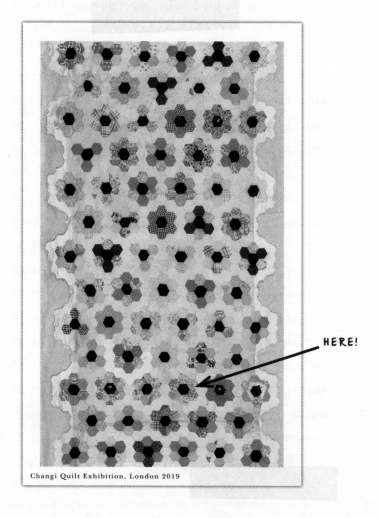

HERE!

Changi Quilt Exhibition, London 2019

29TH MAY, PANCAKES FOR BREAKFAST!

CLOUDS: *Altocumulus stratiformis — very pretty ripples*

Grandma is a pro with Solo. They slept in the same room together and it is now nine o'clock and they are both still asleep! I am sitting at the kitchen table – excuse the grease marks – and Mum is cooking pancakes. This has not happened since the birth of my little, burping brother. Hooray and yum!

Later, Mum and Lilly are going to help me and Harry decorate the inside of Artcloud in "sample-pot stripes", with one wall in blackboard paint for me to draw on. They are also going to rig up a desk for all my art things and a shelf for Harry's cloud-spotting notebooks. I can't wait for it all to be finished.

LATER

Oh dear, you are not going to believe this. Lilly got stuck up in Artcloud – we nearly had to call the fire brigade! Mum and Lilly had finished all the painting, which stinks but looks mega brilliant, and Mum had just reached the bottom of our ladder when Lilly had a meltdown! She said her baby bump was too big and she couldn't get it off the walkway and onto the ladder. Please note, Lilly is three months pregnant, not nine months pregnant – if she does have a baby bump it is invisible to everyone but her! Maybe she is secretly scared of heights.

Anyway, she sat up there for ages sniffling away, until Joe came home. Then he and Harry managed to ease her down between them. What a fuss! I'm not having kids if they make you that useless even before they are born – please note, Harry!

Don't involve me in that conversation, Angie. You're the one who keeps saying that we'll get married one day, not me. And I certainly

never agreed to having kids – I'm not even a
grown-up yet! Over and out, Harry.

Don't listen to him, Diary, he's just embarrassed!

30TH MAY,
A CLOUDLESS DAY

There were no clouds today, which was perfect because it gave Harry and me a chance to settle in to Artcloud. When we got hungry we rang our bell for service and Grandma and Solo made a sandwich delivery via the pulley. Harry keeps nagging Grandma to tell us more about Changi Prison – she says she'll think about it. She has this little box in her bedroom that she brought to show the people at the museum, but she won't tell us what's in it and it's driving Harry mad!

I think it is the skeleton of a Changi rat, with the mangled finger of a prisoner that the rat chewed off one dark and fateful night! –H

Stop rubbishing my diary, Harry.

JUNE

POSSIBLY MY SECOND-BEST MONTH!

- - - - - - - - - - - - - - - - - -

2ND JUNE, BUSY, BUSY, BUSY!

CLOUDS: *Cirrocumulus — high, little patches of cloud — not good for animal spotting*

Dear Diary,

Sorry for the absence, I did warn you that I was a lousy diary keeper. I've been busy doing things and I've not had a spare millisecond. Anyway, some of the things I have been doing have been boring, like homework, cleaning out the fish tank while Edith plays dead, and helping Mum and Grandma with Solo. But mostly I have been having a brilliant time with Harry in Artcloud. It is our secret world and nobody is allowed to come up unless we say so. No adults, no kids and no stinking babies – so no Solo, phew!

It has been totally perfect, except for Harry's head which seems to ache a lot. We think it may be craning his neck to see the clouds, so we have put cloud cushions on the floor. Now we can lie on our backs and look up at the sky, which is loads more comfortable. I like lying down to draw so it suits me.

Grandma Gertie says that if we are really careful she will think about lending us Grandpa Jimmy's very special and amazingly old marine telescope so that we can have a closer look at the clouds and the night sky. Grandma met Grandpa Jimmy when they were both little kids in Changi Prison and Grandpa had the telescope with him then. It was very precious to Grandpa as it had been given to him by his grandfather, which means it must be truly ancient! Harry is beside himself with excitement, but Grandma can take ages thinking things over so I'm not holding my breath – well, maybe just a little. I think it must be the telescope that Grandma has hidden in her secret box. What do you think, Harry?

I told you, it's a dead rat and a mangled finger! –H

Oh, go away you idiot!

LATER

Harry has donated his favourite stuffed owl to Artcloud – stuffed with sweets that he steals from his mum's so-called "secret" store.

I told you not to share my secrets with your diary! Besides, they are usually sweets bought with my own money that Mum has hidden away, so it's not exactly stealing!

I've told you before – keep out of my diary!

Anyway, the owl is looking pretty skinny now because we have spent the afternoon gorging ourselves! Harry was charting different clouds and I was drawing them so we needed the sugar energy.

I turned the clouds into animals. The first was a very rare cirrus cloud called a Kelvin-Helmholtz wave cloud – I've never actually seen one, but Harry says it looks like curling waves. I think it is formed by winds moving in different directions, like sea currents. I drew Harry and me, plus our imaginary dog, riding the waves in our cloud ship!

The second one I drew was my favourite cloud: cumulus. It comes in magical shapes and can be as heavy as a herd of elephants! Cumulus clouds are like shape-shifters – this one went from a giant, to a dog, to a lion, to a bear and then a fish. After that it just floated away as if to say, "That's it, your entertainment is over now and I'm going home for a rest!"

Harry is going to write about clouds, with my permission this time. Here he is

– say hello, Harry.

Hello, Harry and hello, Angie's Diary,
This is the sweet stealer and cloud spotter
extraordinaire, Harry Christmas! My worst
cloud this half term has been nimbostratus.
It is thick and black and covers the whole
sky like a mist in your head. Nimbostratus
won't go away until it's all rained out, which
can take ages. The only good thing about
nimbostratus is that it makes Angie and me
feel that Artcloud is the cosiest and driest
place in the world!
And now back to you, Angie.

Thank you, Harry, and good night – it's
time for hot chocolate with marshmallows.
Yes, more sweets, but don't tell anyone!

3RD JUNE, STAR OF RADIO AND TV, GERTRUDE OLIVE MOON!

CLOUDS: *Cumulus fractus*

Dear Diary,

This has been a seriously great day. Grandma Gertie visited Artcloud, bringing the admission price of two ice creams and her treasure box!

Grandma doesn't like being in small spaces – it reminds her of when she was in Changi Prison. Poor Grandma. The Japanese stuffed over 2,000 prisoners into a little jail meant for only a few hundred people, so it was very, very crowded and claustrophobic. Now small spaces frighten Grandma, which is not surprising! Harry and I felt very honoured by her visit.

We hauled the ice creams and treasure box up in the pulley, while Grandma bravely mounted the ladder to our little cloud land.

After we'd eaten the ice creams and shown her around, which took all of two minutes, she opened the box and brought out my Grandpa Jimmy's marine telescope! It is made of green leather and shiny brass. It is tiny when it's folded up, but it looks very impressive when you pull it out – like something from a pirate film.

Grandma said we could borrow it for cloud spotting. Yes, she really, really did. Since Grandpa Jimmy died, it has been her most treasured possession so I am gobsmacked and Harry is double gobsmacked! Grandpa Jimmy managed to keep his telescope hidden from the prison guards all through the war. He also helped Grandma hide the letters she wrote to her kitten, Rosie!

The letters that haven't vanished or rotted away now live in the box with the telescope and a couple of old newspaper clippings that Grandpa Jimmy must have stuffed in there just before the war. The paper the letters are written on is very, very fragile and might just crumble away so Grandma wouldn't let us touch them, but she said she'd ask Dad to get them copied and then she might read them to us. In the meantime, she suggested we make a patchwork quilt for Artcloud, full of our memories, like the one she made in Changi. I thought it was a crepuscular idea, but Harry wasn't so sure – I don't think he knows what sewing needles are for!

Yes I do, they're for pricking annoying girls with!

4TH JUNE, THE FIRST ROSIE LETTER

CLOUDS: *Cumulus humilis*

Dear Diary,

I hate to over-indulge you with too many entries, but the truth is life is so exciting I've just got to tell you about it! Dad copied Grandma's Rosie letters last night and today Harry and I persuaded her to read us the first one. It is truly incredible and luckily Dad made two copies so that I can stick one into your pages.

When Grandma starts on the letters she seems to remember every moment of that time as if it was yesterday. She says the first letter was written just after the island of Singapore had surrendered to the Japanese. Nobody had expected the invasion and nobody knew what was going to happen, least of all poor Grandma. Grandma's dad had left their house two days earlier to try to get the family passage on a ship back to England. He didn't return and Grandma and her mum were frightened he'd been captured or killed – how scary that must have been.

This is my copy of the first letter. The actual, actual letter is all smudged with age and a bit torn.

17th FEBRUARY, 1942
THE CRICKET GROUND, SINGAPORE

Dear Kitten Rosie,

You are the very best kitten in the whole world and you were my very best eighth birthday present. Just this morning you were curled up on my lap with blue ribbon around your neck - now I don't know where you are. I know where I am and it's terrible. I'm sitting on a cricket pitch surrounded by Japanese soldiers with guns and bayonets. I'm scared and miserable, first I lost Daddy and now you. Mummy says I'm not to let the soldiers see me cry, so I won't cry even though I want to. I will try to get back home to you, Rosie, very, very soon.

I think we are at war with the Japanese because there has been lots of bombing in Singapore and Japanese soldiers marching everywhere, but nobody tells me anything. Today the soldiers ordered all women and children to come and sit on this cricket pitch - there are hundreds of us. There is no shade and it is a boiling hot day. Mummy is nearly passing out because she is wearing four dresses! We had half an hour to leave our home and get here. Mummy made me wear three dresses, four pairs of knickers, two pairs of socks and my hat. I tried to hide you in my satchel, but she found you and chased you out of the house — I'm sorry. Please find somewhere safe to live until I can come and find you. Whatever you do, don't let the soldiers get you.

I've got to go now, the soldiers are taking everyone's precious things. I must hide my paper and pencil or I won't be able to write to you again. They're hitting people with their rifles. I am so, so frightened. Mummy is crying even though she said not to. I wish my daddy was here.

Purrs and strokes, Gertie. XXXX

Isn't that incredible? It's like a story in a book. We had to beg Grandma to read the next letter, because she was all choked up, but after a little pause she was off again!

Dear Kitten Rosie,

We've been here for ages. I'm frightened that if I'm seen writing I might get killed. They killed a Chinese woman just now and all because she gave an old lady some water. I covered Peter's eyes so he wouldn't see, 'cos he's only four. The soldiers tipped out my satchel looking for valuables - or radios and cameras that I might use for spying. My doll, Olga, fell out and the soldiers trampled her into the ground - imagine if it had been you, Rosie. I'm trying to bury poor Olga under the turf, but it's tricky without being seen.

The boy in front of me hid something under his hat, so I did the same with my paper and pencil. Mummy had our money hidden in her shoe, but they found that. Now we've got nothing but some sewing needles, two tins of condensed milk, a jar of Marmite and what we're wearing. I hope they don't search us again. The boy in front has big blue eyes and blond, curly hair. He looks like an angel, which means they probably won't search him because angels don't hide things - unlike girls with straight, mousy hair. Oh Rosie, I wish you were here, even though you can be a bit scratchy.

Purrs and strokes,

A very scared Gertie

Don't you think my grandma was brave, hiding her paper and pencil under her hat? I'm not sure I'd be brave enough to hide you under my hat, Diary!

Harry and I wanted to read more but Grandma wanted to go and help with Solo. I think she found reading about such a sad time really difficult. I do love my grandma – she's historic! I think we should definitely get her to help us make a patchwork quilt for Artcloud. Hold on – Harry's got the writing bug!

I think Gertie was fantastically brave too. She's altogether pretty cool for an ancient – a bit of a crepuscular ray! As for borrowing the telescope – that is totally awesome and I am lost for words! Apart from seeing clouds and stars better, we can spy on our neighbours. I might even agree to help make a patchwork quilt, as long as it has lots of clouds on it and I only have to cut the hexagons and advise.

Grandma said Artcloud felt really cosy

and not a bit like Changi. She intends to be a regular visitor, if we agree – which we might for the sake of the letters, help with quilt-making and lots of ice cream treats!

5TH JUNE,
MY MISSING FRIEND

Dear Diary,

Don't ask me about the clouds today, because I don't care. Clouds are a Harry thing and I'm off all Harry things. We were supposed to go back to school together after half term, but when I knocked for Harry there was no answer. I thought maybe he'd forgotten and gone on without me, but here I am in the playground with no Harry, just my diary! All those grunge girls tease me when Harry's not about. "Lost your twin?" "Don't your boyfriend love you no more?" I'll kill him when I get home, I truly will.

LATER — IN ARTCLOUD

I came straight out here after school and rang the bell three times, meaning "Come quick, I need you urgently," but the lazy hedgehog didn't come. I'm really, really cross. Yes I flipping am, really, really cross. Poor Grandma

Gertie, she'll regret lending us the telescope if Harry has lost interest in it already!

Just finished my homework and rung the bell again – still no Harry. He must be at home now, because I can see his mum in the kitchen. What's the matter with him? Mum's calling, so I'll have to go.

LATER STILL – IN BED

Dearest Diary,

I wish I could rub all my crossness out but it's written in ink so it's there to stay. Harry is not being mean, he's ill. I think he may be very ill, but there is just a lot of whispering and nobody is quite saying. His mum took him to the doctor this morning because of his headaches and being sick. It turns out it's not craning his neck or eating too many sausages. The doctor sent them straight to the hospital where Harry had loads of tests. He's at home asleep now. Lilly says I can go and see him before school tomorrow. I'm going to wake up really early and study the clouds so that I can tell him all about them.

6TH JUNE,
A NOT GOOD DAY

I don't know what's going on. I went to see Harry before school, but his dad wouldn't let me in. When I gave him the cloud card I'd drawn for Harry he gave me a big hug, which was weird as hugging is not a Joe thing.

LATER

Harry's gone back to hospital. I'm freaked out, people die in hospitals!

9TH JUNE, A VERY NOT GOOD DAY

Dear and very special Diary,

Suddenly, I am really glad to have you to talk to. Now I see why people keep a diary and it's not to report on the day, it's to give your true heart and feelings a place to explode. Well, here's my explosion, which is made up of little crystals of sadness and fear: boom, crash, smash and splinter! I'm like a cumulonimbus thundercloud, or maybe like the Japanese god of thunder and lightning, Raiden. He looks like a red devil, has sharp claws and likes eating human belly buttons – gross.

The last days have been like a terrible dream. I want to cry all the time, which is really dumb and selfish because I'm the lucky one. It's not me that's ill, it's Harry, and he is very ill. Mum says that doctors are clever people and they'll make him better, but that feels

THESE ARE **NOT** KISSES — THEY ARE CROSSES COS I WISH I COULD CROSS THESE DAYS OUT OF **EXISTENCE!!!**

slippery to me. I keep imagining this terrible space opening up where Harry should be, but isn't. A bit like when you're drawing a cloud and it vanishes before you've finished – just the empty sky remains. I am so scared, I can't imagine life without Harry. He's always been there, always, always.

Now I know why Grandma likes to be at home with Grandpa Jimmy's things, because I just want to wrap myself in Artcloud among Harry's things. I hid up there after school, but Grandma found me. She clambered up the ladder with a pocket full of hexagons. She says that she'll help me do the sewing, but I have to design the quilt myself because I'm the artist in the family. She says to pack it full of jokes and memories to surprise Harry with. I've started drawing ideas already. It makes me feel better to be doing something for Harry. I wonder if Grandma writes about making the Changi quilt in her letters to Rosie, and if making the quilt made her feel better. Grandma's going to read us some more letters when Harry comes home so maybe I'll find out.

10ᵀᴴ JUNE,
THE HOSPITAL

I haven't seen Harry since half term, but I am going
to the hospital today. I feel nervous, but bursting
to see him. I need to tell him that he's got to get
better. He can be so flicking lazy, he might just do
a hedgehog hibernation and not bother if I don't
nag him. I'm going to draw him another cloud
card now.

LATER

I thought Harry might have changed into some
horrible hospital monster – but he was still
Harry, only maybe a bit smaller and whiter.
He is in a room on his own with an extra
bed for his mum. He was in bed when we got
there, but quite chatty. Mum took Lilly for
a cup of tea so Harry and I had a chance to
talk. I told him he had to work at getting
better, but he didn't answer. He wants me to
bring in some sweets tomorrow, and also his
cloud notebook and some more of Grandma

Gertie's Rosie letters, but I don't think she'll like that. Then a nurse came to take some blood, so I had to go. Well, I didn't have to go, but needles make me feel funny.

SECRET: I have just snuck out to Artcloud and emptied our owl store of sweets. They're hidden in my backpack now, along with Harry's latest cloud-spotting notebook. I hope I don't get caught, because I don't think you're allowed sweets in hospital. I didn't dare ask Grandma about the letters. I'll wait a bit.

11TH JUNE, ANOTHER HOSPITAL VISIT

Grandma took me to hospital today as Mum was busy with Solo and cooking for Harry's dad. It was boiling hot but Grandma was wearing at least three scarves – she's daft! She bought me a doughnut with sprinkles for a snack and no cucumber sticks – what would Mum say!

We got a bus straight to the hospital, but when we arrived Harry wasn't in his room. The nurse said he was having tests, so we waited. When he came back he was in a wheelchair and wouldn't talk to us. I think he was embarrassed.

Grandma went to the cafe with Lilly while I stayed with Harry. He cheered up a bit when he saw the sweets and his notebook. He took all the red sweets and hid them under his pillow. Then he wrote this note on the pad by his bed:

CUMULONIMBUS –
GO AWAY!

With that he turned to the wall and fell asleep – so rude! But cumulonimbus is a really bad storm cloud, which means that Harry was not feeling at all good.

I didn't know what to do, so I sat in silence and drew a picture of a cumulonimbus cloud – well, how I think it looks. If Harry was awake he would have said it's the King of Clouds and can grow to ten miles high. It is often the shape of an anvil, which mine was – sort of!

Lilly and Grandma came back and we were just about to leave when Harry opened his eyes and asked Grandma if she was going to read a Rosie letter or not. He was so rude, he didn't even say please. I thought she'd be really cross, but she just took a letter out of her bag and started reading. Good old Grandma!

18th FEBRUARY, 1942
CHANGI PRISON

Dearest, bestest Kitten Rosie,

I have so much to tell you! After the soldiers searched us yesterday we had to start marching. We had nothing to eat or drink all day and were very hungry and thirsty. Children were crying, women fainting and the soldiers barking, but on and on we marched. Mummy tried to help me, but she could hardly manage herself and Peter. The boy with the hat and the blond hair was burnt red by the sun. My mouth was dust dry and flies were climbing up my nostrils.

After hours of marching we stopped in front of the gates of Changi Prison! I knew it was Changi because we have a beach hut nearby — we were there on holiday just a few weeks ago. I never dreamed I'd be a prisoner inside the jail, Rosie, because I'm not a bad person! I wonder what they did with all the old prisoners? I hope they're not hiding somewhere.

I wanted to cry when the gates opened, but all the women started singing "There'll Always Be An England" and we went through without any tears. Then there was another iron gate, but before we went through it I glimpsed my daddy! Yes, really, really, I'm sure it was. He was behind a wall with some other men and they were all waving through a grille. The soldiers wouldn't let us stop and Mummy says it was my imagination, but it wasn't. He's not dead, Rosie, and you mustn't be either!

Through the second iron gate there were rows and rows of cells. They are only just big enough to lie down in, with a concrete bed in the middle and a concrete pillow. There's a tiny grille window and a hole in the floor for a toilet. Tonight we are sharing with a lady and her little nephew. They are sleeping on the concrete bed, with me on one side and Mummy and Peter on the other. I feel ever so hungry and lonely. I'm not sure when I'll see you again, Rosie. Mummy says it won't be long because we're bound to be rescued.
I hope she's right.
Good night, purrs and love, Gertie xxx

PS The lady in the concrete bed thinks we'll all be killed if I get caught writing. She says the guards will think I'm a spy. I'll find a hiding place tomorrow where I can save your letters until I can post them.
PPS I'm really, really scared.

Just imagine, Diary – if that had been me I wouldn't have been able to write in you without risking my life! That is a truly fearful thought.

I wanted to talk to Harry about it, but he had fallen asleep and so had Lilly. Grandma and I crept out. I hate not being able to talk about every single little thing with Harry, it's just something I've always, always done. I cried a smidgen when we left and Grandma hugged me close. She told me that when she was in Changi Prison she had at least eight really bad attacks of malaria. Once she was so ill the carpenter made her a coffin. There was no medicine and the doctor could do nothing but drip water into her mouth. They were sure Gertie would die. Well, she didn't. She surprised everyone by recovering, and the coffin went to waste!

"And the moral of that tale," said Grandma Gertie, "is never give up on someone!"

I asked her if we could read Harry some more Rosie letters next time we visit, because he really loves listening to them. She said we could. I won't ever give up on Harry and nor will Grandma. She's going to ask Mum if she can stay until he's better – I hope she can. Grandma's also going to ask Mum for some cotton scraps for our quilt – great!

LATER

I didn't feel like visiting Artcloud this evening. It doesn't seem the same without Harry – it's spidery and lonesome. Anyway, Solo was crying so Mum gave him to me to jiggle. I must have the knack, because he was soon asleep. I suppose he's quite sweet really. He wouldn't let go of my finger so we watched telly together until Mum sent me up to bed. Good night, Harry, get better soon. I'll visit you again tomorrow.

INNERMOST SECRET THOUGHT: Grandma wouldn't have said she'd stay until Harry's better if she didn't believe he will get better... Would she?

Question: Did I remember to feed Edith today?

Answer: Glug, bubble, glug! (In case you were wondering, that's fish for "Not finning enough!")

P.S. Drawing usually cheers me up, but today I've been too sad to draw anything, even Edith.

12TH JUNE,
A NOTHING,
NO HARRY DAY

I am writing this under my bed with various dirty socks, pants, fluff balls and books. Grandma knocked on my door to ask if she could show me some of the cotton for our quilt, but I don't want to talk to anyone – not Mum, not Dad, not Grandma and definitely not Solo.

I wasn't allowed to visit Harry today. Mum said he needed to rest. What was almost worse was that nobody teased me at school. I guess everyone has been told that Harry is really, really ill. They've given some kid called Peter Maudle his part in the play. I bet he doesn't sing as well as Harry. I haven't got a part at all, but I don't care because I'm going to be looking out for Harry.

BUT I CAN'T DO THAT IF I'M NOT EVEN ALLOWED TO FLIPPING VISIT HIM!

13TH JUNE, THIRTEEN IS NOT AN UNLUCKY NUMBER

CLOUDS: *On cloud nine - which means I am very happy and sitting on a cumulonimbus cloud after the storm has passed. It is the tallest of all cloud types and was numbered nine in the first ever* International Cloud Atlas *published in 1896— oh shut up, Angie, before you become as nerdy about clouds as Harry!*

MORNING – IN ARTCLOUD

Well, Harry is the reason I'm on cloud nine: he has been allowed home and I've been allowed a day off school – hooray! He has got pills to stop his head aching and other pills to stop him being sick. He seems really cheerful. He says that doctors have pills for everything!

Anyway, Harry should be cheery because his mum and dad say that he can have a puppy after he's had an operation to make his head better! I'm really pleased that he's having an operation because Grandma says that surgeons only operate if they think it will help someone recover. I am jealous he's going to get a puppy though – Mum would never let me have one. Actually, I can't believe it because Harry's mum doesn't even like dogs and she's about to have a baby. She must have gone soppy in the head. Are you reading this over my shoulder, Harry Christmas?

Hi Angie's Diary,
Yes, I blinkin' am! It's true, I am getting a
puppy and Mum has never thought much
of dogs, but she says it's to bribe me to get
better. I want Angie to share the puppy with
me, just in case the operation doesn't work
– which it will. Angie and I can choose and
name the puppy together. The vet knows of
a litter of mutts and we are going to go and
pick ours soon! How crepuscular is that? They
were only born last week so we can't bring
it home, just pick the cutest of the litter –
snuffle, yap, lick!
 Over and out, Harry

Well, all I can say is that you can't be ill if you've got a dog to look after.

I won't be, Angie. After my operation I'm giving up headaches, vomiting, blood tests and hospitals! My word is my bond.
Yours, Harry Christmas

AFTERNOON

Mum made Harry's favourite cake and I decorated it. Grandma Gertie and I took it out to Artcloud and hauled it up! Then we rang the bell twice. I knew Harry would be pleased to have cake, along with another Rosie letter – and he was!

Grandma has put all the letters in order now. She says they don't tell the whole story of her time in Changi Prison, but more than enough. She asked Harry if he'd like to read a letter to us, but we like it when Grandma reads them, because they sound proper old-fashioned and we can close our eyes and imagine.

19th FEBRUARY, 1942 — CHANGI PRISON
MUM WAS WRONG, NOBODY HAS RESCUED US.

Dear Kitten Rosie,

I don't know if that was my daddy yesterday. The men and the boys from ten years up are in another part of the jail. We can't see them, talk to them or send messages. I'm so miserable and scared — I just want to come home to you, bestest kitten.

We have an English camp commander now, Doctor Lake — she's very bossy! She found some rusty witches' cauldrons and made us children scrub them with stones until the rust was gone — it took all day. Luckily, I made friends with the boy in the hat. He's called Jimmy and he's nine years old.

It turns out he put a telescope under his hat. It's hidden now and deadly secret so I better not say any more or I might get Jimmy killed.

The guards gave us all a bag of rice to share, but we don't know how long it has to last. Mummy cooked it in the cauldrons, but she wouldn't give me and Peter extra because that wouldn't be fair. Anyway, it has insects in it!

Have you still got the wool ball I made for you Rosie?

Love you,

Purrs and strokes from a very hungry Gertie

This is such a sad letter, poor little Grandma. If I'd been her, I'd have put those Japanese guards in the cauldrons and boiled them up instead of the buggy rice. Grandma must have had enough to worry about in Changi without worrying about Rosie too. She says she thought of Rosie every day right to the end, but she never did work out a way to post her letters. The Red Cross used to deliver some letters for people in the prison, but Grandma was too scared to ask them to deliver letters to a kitten!

Harry was curled up and asleep by the end of the letter. Grandma covered him with a blanket and then she and I lay on our backs and looked for kittens in the clouds. We decided to add Kitten Rosie to the quilt. Grandma and I have almost worked out the quilt design and Grandma says we can add the rest as we go along. Mum has cut scraps from lots of my old clothes that she was saving in case Lilly has a baby girl, but they'll look much better in our quilt. We're going to start sewing this evening!

18TH JUNE, HARRY STEALS MY DIARY!

HARRY REPORTING ON CLOUDS AND LIFE:

A CIRRUS CLOUD DAY!

If Angie hasn't already told you, cirrus means a curly lock of hair in Latin, and cirrus clouds are usually very like wisps of hair. They are quite high and "point" to fair weather. I feel fair weather MUST be on the way because ... we chose my puppy today! Angie thinks he's her puppy – but she's so wrong! He's as cute as a cloud but a lot smaller. You write the rest, Angie, I'm not big on words just puppies and clouds.

Oh my dizzy Diary,

I am writing this after the most awesome morning. Like Harry said, we went to choose his/my puppy. The litter was only ten days old, but they were the cutest things you've ever seen. We chose the smallest boy puppy. He is the colour of a fox and has a pink, speckled nose and one white paw. He now has a blue ribbon around his neck so that everyone knows he's Harry's – and a little bit mine! We chose blue because Kitten Rosie had a blue ribbon on when Grandma was given her. He will definitely be featuring on our quilt!

We are inviting Grandma up to Artcloud to help choose a name for him. We are each going to put three names in a hat and then pick one out. Harry has the final say though – or so he thinks!

LATER

Harry had to have a rest and so did Grandma. Grandma has had a dicky heart for years on account of the terrible conditions and lack of food in Changi Prison. While they rested Dad and I started to paint the outside of Artcloud. It is wild. The house is red with a dark blue roof and then the walkway is blue and white, like a floating cloud in the tree!

By teatime I was sick of painting so I rang the Artcloud bell for Harry and Grandma. A few minutes later Harry's nose appeared at the top of his ladder and Grandma's at the top of ours – result! We put the puppy names into the sweet owl and shook them up, then we left them to stew while Gertie read us the next Rosie letter.

SECRET: Sometimes I wish Grandma wouldn't read any more letters because they are just too sad. But I know how special they are, and how much they mean to her and Harry.

5th APRIL, 1942

STILL IN JAIL - STILL UNRESCUED.

Dearest Kitten Rosie,

Still here, miserable and hungry - it is hateful. The guards are horrid to us, every morning they make us stand in the exercise yard to be counted. After that we have to bow to the Japanese flag and sing their anthem - it takes ages and people faint in the heat. If we don't bow whenever we see a guard they kick us, or hit us with a rifle butt. We have to knit hats for them. Mine are full of holes - good.

I go to prison school now, which is run by some of the prisoners. The Japanese won't let us learn things like history and geography, so we mostly do sums, dancing and sports. Jimmy is good at everything and everyone likes him, he's such a smiler!

I like school, but best of all I like the Girl Guides and our lovely Guide leader, Miss Elizabeth. Even Changi doesn't feel so bad when we are with her. There are twenty Guides and I'm the youngest. Mummy has lent us her needles so that we can embroider our badges. I am going to try to earn my wildflower badge first. Even though I'm the youngest, I'm one of the best sewers. The nuns who taught us in my old school were very keen on our writing and needlework - I even won prizes!

We forgot to bring toothbrushes and toothpaste. Mummy's in a right old tizzy and says our teeth will fall out, but I clean mine with my finger. Mummy washes Peter's and my clothes in the shower, but I have to wear my knickers for a whole week – or more! The drains go through to the men's camp and we can hear them moving about, but I still don't know for sure if my daddy is there.

We are all so hungry we are starting to look like little rice grains.

The Guides might make Miss Elizabeth a patchwork quilt as a surprise present. We think we might be able to beg little scraps of cotton when people's clothes rot in the sun. Then we can sew them together and make a beautiful pattern. I hope so. It'll be scary though, because the guards don't like us gathering in groups.

Purrs and strokes from your very best friend,
Gertie

PS Don't forget me, Rosie, and don't starve to death. Please don't.
PPS I hate wearing the same knickers for a week – Mummy says not to fuss.

It was exciting to read about the very start of the quilt. That last bit about the knickers sent me and Harry into fits of giggles because of my secret nickname! It is hard to believe that anyone would lock a little girl up in a prison. I wouldn't mind not having to clean my teeth though!

After Grandma had read the letter we decided our puppy names were well enough stewed. Harry put his hand in, stirred them around, ate a sweet or two, stirred them around again and then picked. Out came one from Grandma – Knickers! We all got the giggles again. Sometimes I think Grandma Gertie is younger than us, not a million years older! Harry picked again and out came my favourite, Cirrus – and Harry said YES. So he is now officially Puppy Cirrus!

After that Grandma fell asleep and Harry asked me to do something so scary I can't even write it down – at least not yet. I just don't know if I dare do it, but Harry got cross when I said that. He looked through the telescope and wouldn't talk any more, the silent, stubborn hedgehog.

I've got to shut my eyes to think about this. The thing is, Harry has to go into hospital tomorrow to prepare for his operation. They have to do lots of tests before they operate, because operating on your head is a tricky business. I know it's not nice for him, but I still don't know if he should've asked me to do such a difficult thing. I just couldn't say yes straight out, not even to my almost-twin.

I'm only going to think about Harry being better, because as soon as he is we are going to visit Cirrus again! If he's talking to me by then – Harry I mean, not Cirrus.

I think I might do that thing Harry asked. He said if it was the other way round he'd do it for me – except I wouldn't let him. I've got to sleep on it. Good night.

19TH JUNE,
I HATE HARRY – YOU
BETTER BELIEVE IT!

CLOUDS: *Don't even mention clouds!*

Dear Diary,

This is a really big secret: if I wasn't so worried that Harry might die I would really, really hate him at the moment! I woke up this morning to wild shouts and screams. Harry has only flicking well climbed onto the roof of Artcloud and is refusing to come down! What an idiot – he could get one of his headaches, turn dizzy and fall. Isn't it enough that he's ill without risking death by falling?

I ran into the garden to give him what for! I double hate Harry now. When I went outside he dropped a note wrapped around a stone down to me.

This is it:

NOT KISSES!

74

I don't like you and your knickers stink!
You've got to agree or I'll never come down,
I'll just sit up here and starve to death.
Then you'll be sorry... Also I will never ever
let you see Cirrus 'cos he's my puppy
and not yours.
You are unfriended - Harry

It's not right, it's blackmail. I've a good mind
to cut down the ladders so Harry can't ever
get up to Artcloud again.

I will do what he asked, but I don't want to.

LATER

This has been one dumb day! Harry finally
climbed down and has gone back to hospital.
I am at school with my backpack full of
"things" for Harry. My stomach is a mass of
footballing butterflies and I can't even think
about school work. Grandma promised to
collect me after school and take me to visit
Harry, but I hope she forgets. I don't even care
about not having a doughnut with sprinkles,

which is definitely my preferred after-school snack, permitted only by Grandma.

MUCH LATER – FROM UNDER MY BED

This is not good, none of this is good and now everyone is shouting and crying, which makes it even worse! As if I didn't know that what I did was wrong, but I've got to stand by Harry no matter what. I want to cry, but I won't because I've got to write this.

The stupid doctor told Harry that they would have to shave off his hair before the operation and he was really scared by that – don't ask me why. Anyway, he asked me to do it for him. He said it'd be like when we were little and used to play hairdressers – I don't think so!

Well, as you know, I decided I'd have to stick by Harry and do it. So I took Dad's razor, shaving foam and some scissors to school, hidden in the bottom of my backpack. When we got to the hospital Grandma and Lilly went for a coffee, and me and Harry locked ourselves in the bathroom. First I snipped off all his hair, which was quite fun really.

The floor shimmered gold and he looked more like a hedgehog than ever. Then I covered his head in Dad's shaving foam, which was also fun, and shaved the stubble off, which was scary and horrid! I did nick him with the razor a few times and he ended up with a few bloody patches, but not too many.

We flushed all Harry's hair down the loo, which was pretty pointless since the nurses weren't about to stick it back on! Harry said I was the best friend anyone could have and if he died I could have Cirrus. Which was just stupid, because I didn't shave his flicking head just so he could die!

The rest is a blur and not a very happy one. When Lilly saw what I'd done to Harry's head she wouldn't stop screaming and crying. Grandma had to ring Harry's dad and ask him to come and look after her. We never got to read the next Rosie letter because Grandma had to take me home double quick.

Grandma's gone to bed now and no one else is talking to me, except Solo who smiled at me and did a double burp. He's not a bad little brother, I suppose.

EVEN LATER

I couldn't sleep so I have been sitting up in bed tacking some of the cotton onto hexagons for the quilt. It's ever so soothing and it helps you think. I may tell you what I've been thinking in the morning – or I may not.

20TH JUNE,
ALMOST-TWINS STICK
TOGETHER

CLOUDS: *Contrails but no clouds*

EARLY MORNING – ARTCLOUD

I'm not upset any more. I've had a think and that think says I did right. Harry is my very best friend and almost-twin – sometimes you've just got to do things, no matter what. So I've shaved my own hair off in sympathy. I don't half look a freak, but what's right for Harry is right for his almost-twin! Nobody thought to take the shaving stuff out of my backpack yesterday, so I came up to Artcloud before anyone was awake and just did it. It looks a bit of a mess, because you need a friend to get at the back bits, but... Well actually, I just look a total oddball.

I'm stuck in Artcloud now, because I'm too scared to show myself. But I'm not going to cry about it, even though I feel like it, because

Harry should not go through this alone.

LATER

Dad came to fetch me down from Artcloud. He did a double and triple blink when he saw me. Then he hugged me tight and said I was outstandingly brave and a very good friend – but he had better go and warn Mum, Gertie and Solo or the shock might be too much for them.

Dad was gone for a very long time, but finally he came back and dragged me down and into the house. When I went into the kitchen I could tell Mum had been crying, but everyone cheered. Even Harry's dad was there and gave me his second ever hug!

I'm not to go into school today, but I'm going to see Harry. His operation is tomorrow and everyone thinks that it will do him good to see his bald twin. Mum shaved off the strands of hair at the back and I tried on different hats for the journey – a woolly one looks best, even though it's too hot for June!

Mum is going to stay with Solo so Grandma

is taking me. We are going to make a day of it
and take the telescope and the Rosie letters.
Joe says we will have to wait outside if Harry's
with the doctor, but that we can hang out in
the hospital all day. Grandma has bagged up all
our patchwork quilt bits and we are going to
take it with us. Even if Harry doesn't want
to join in, Grandma and I intend to distract
ourselves with sewing when Harry is having
tests or seeing the doctors.

STLL LATER — HOSPITAL
OK Diary,

I know I look weird but I don't care any more.
When Harry saw me he rolled out of bed
with laughter and he hasn't laughed like
that since we read about Grandma's knickers!
The nurse came in and burst out laughing too —
she said that I was better than any medicine.
Harry's asleep now and so is Gertie, but I'm
happy because we have had a wicked morning.

After Harry and I had compared bald heads,
Grandma told us that in Changi there was no
need to shave heads because there was so

little food your hair just fell out. Lilly went home to get some clean things and rest her baby bump. When we were alone, Grandma gave Harry the telescope so that he could watch the clouds from his bed. He was as chuffed as anything and begged her to read one more letter. She said she'd have to think about it, but she was only teasing because in the end she read two letters in a row! All the time Grandma was reading, Harry was clutching on to the telescope and my hand – it felt like when we were little.

1st MAY, 1942

Dearest Kitten Rosie,

It's getting hard to write to you because more people are arriving all the time and everywhere is so crowded. A mother with three children was put into our cell – it was such a squeeze that Mummy moved us into a passage. The guards walk past us in the night and I'm frightened they'll find my letters. Sometimes they kick our beds just for fun.

A terrible thing happened yesterday. A little boy was playing in the dirt near two guards when they suddenly accused him of eavesdropping – even though he couldn't speak Japanese. The next second they had chopped his ear off and it was lying in the dust. The poor blighter was so shocked he didn't even cry.

If they find my letters they might chop my hand off, or even kill me. But writing to you, Guiding and looking at the stars and clouds with Jimmy – even though we can't use the "you-know-what" – is all I've got. Jimmy knows the names of every cloud and every constellation.

Purrs and strokes,
Gertie

20th JULY, 1942

Dearest Kitten Rosie,
Exciting news: even though the guards
are always so cross with us, the
Guides are definitely going to make
Miss Elizabeth a patchwork quilt.
We've found a tiny cell where we can
meet in secret. If we hear the guards
coming we will hide our sewing in
our knickers and pretend we're doing
our lessons!

   I cut the hem from two of my
dresses to make part of my patchwork
rosette. I did it while Mummy was
cooking, because she'd be angry if she found
out. I was really careful to pull the
hemming thread first so I could use it
to sew the hexagons together. A Chinese
woman has given us some black fabric
for the centre rosette. We may never
finish the quilt because it's so hard
to find enough thread and fabric,
but we're determined to try!

Strokes and purrs,
Seamstress Gertie xxx

Harry and I both gave Grandma a hug when she'd finished – her eyes were ever so watery. She said she was tired.

Dear Angie's Diary,
I just want to say that I've got two of the best mates ever and that Angie looks a worse freak than me with no hair! If I wasn't wearing a hospital robe with no back I'd bounce up and down on my bed in honour of my bald friend! Over and out, Harry

LATER – AT HOME IN BED

We left the hospital early because Harry had to go for more tests. I didn't want to leave, because I don't know when I'll see him again.

Before we left, Grandma told us that when things got bad at Changi she and Jimmy used to lie on their backs and imagine floating over the walls on a cloud. She told Harry that for the next few days he would be floating on a cloud. Then his head would start getting better and the cloud would land him gently back on his bed. I think it made us both feel a bit happier.

Tomorrow Dad is taking me to see Cirrus. I'm going to take a photo for Harry, and give Cirrus one of Harry's old sweaters so he'll know Harry's stinky old smell when he next sees him. Dogs are big on smells!

21ˢᵀ JUNE,
OPERATION DAY

CLOUDS: *Nimbostratus - Harry's
least favourite. Grey, gloomy and pouring rain.*

Dearest Diary,

It is late and I don't really feel like writing.
We haven't heard about the operation and may
not have any news until tomorrow. I sent
thought messages all through the day. Usually I
send thoughts on the clouds, but nimbostratus
is too static to carry messages so I had to
make do with telepathy.

I was allowed one more day off school to
go and see Cirrus and buy a new hat to cover
my bald head. It's weird being hairless because
everyone thinks you must be really ill. They
either stare at you or shoot sympathetic
glances at your mum. If they do that to Harry
I'll punch them – baldies would rather not be
noticed is what I reckon. It was hard choosing
a hat but I settled on a baseball cap.

I don't regret shaving my head, but I wish I hadn't had to.

After hat shopping we went to see Cirrus and took some more pictures for Harry. He is so adorable and very clever. He recognised me at once and wagged his little stumpy tail when I picked him up. I don't think he cared that I've got no hair! Dogs are good at not judging you by your looks.

Grandma and I did some more on the patchwork quilt. She helped me sew a cloud hexagon for Harry. I think he'll like it. Grandma says we can sew all his favourite clouds, but that would mean every cloud in the sky, and just sewing one was hard enough! Maybe if I sew all the clouds that Harry has taught me into the quilt it will help Harry get better? I don't know.

Today freaked me out – everyone was super nice, but that's meaningless unless Harry gets better. What if his operation doesn't work? What if, what if, what if?

22ND JUNE,
BACK TO SCHOOL

CLOUDS: *Stratocumulus cumulogenitus*

Dearest Diary,

I went back to school today. I hate, hate, hate it without Harry. We had class assembly and old Lemonpops told everyone about Harry and why I had no hair. Nobody teased me, and the grungy girls said I could hang out with them until Harry is back in school.

At lunchtime Mum came to see me. I felt sick when I saw her. I couldn't think why she would come unless something terrible had happened. It turned out to be really good news, but I still wanted to cry – relief is mega weird. The surgery went well and Harry is in intensive care. He may be there for a few days. We can't visit him until he's back in his room.

Even though he's safe for now, I can't help feeling that a gap is cracking open. Nothing feels really secure any more – it all seems slippery.

At home I collaged a whole quilt square with Harry's favourite sweets, because if I was allowed to visit him that's what I'd take him. Grandma is tacking fabric onto hexagons and squares as though there is no tomorrow. She told me that making the quilt in Changi stopped her and her friends from dwelling on the bad things all the time. It doesn't stop me. Well, maybe just a little.

P.S. Joe brought Grandpa Jimmy's telescope back from the hospital because he was worried about it getting lost. Grandma and I wish Harry had it under his pillow.

24TH JUNE,
STUPID HOSPITAL RULES

CLOUDS: *More stratocumulus*

Hello Diary,

I've got nothing to say to you really. It's the weekend and we're still not allowed to visit Harry. How stupid is that?

Very.

I have been decorating Artcloud ready for Harry's return. I've put up bunting, filled a vase with dried flowers, put a cloth over the table and hung pictures on the wall. I've even hung little curtains over the spy holes. I hope Harry likes it. I think I might ask Grandma to help me make a cloud bed for Cirrus – I can't wait to see Cirrus again.

Grandma came up the ladder with an ice cream treat for me, but I hadn't the heart to eat it without Harry. Grandma didn't mind, she ate it herself! Then she sat and sewed while I drew some of my best memories onto the hexagons for her to embroider. They all include Harry – bouncing on beds, bad jokes, his farts, giggling at grown-ups, stealing sweets from his mum's secret drawer... Whoops, I hope this quilt isn't going to give away all our secrets!

25TH JUNE,
A VISIT TO HARRY!

CLOUDS: *A cloudless day*

Dear Diary,

I went to see Harry today! He was whiter than the bed sheets, his head was just one big bandage and there were drips and tubes everywhere – it freaked me out. He didn't talk, but when I stroked his hand he grabbed on to my finger, like little Solo. The nurse said that Harry was fine, just sleepy because of the drugs, and he would be his old self in no time. I told him about decorating Artcloud, sewing the quilt and that being bald was rubbish without him, so he'd better come home soon. I don't know if he heard me.

In the afternoon Grandma took to her bed and Dad, Mum, Solo and I went rollerblading! It was wicked – Dad was pushing Solo in his buggy and he was squealing with laughter. I was moving so fast that nobody had a chance to stare at me. Then we got pizzas and came home to watch a movie. Grandma fell asleep over the quilt and snored so loudly we could hardly hear a thing. I sewed one whole hexagon all by myself and wonky it is not!

SECRET: Dad and I are sleeping in Artcloud tonight. It is only a secret because we think Harry might have wanted to be the first to spend the whole night out here. We've got a feast, but Dad's fallen asleep – everyone is always falling asleep!

I'm going to lie on my back and look up at the stars. Harry would love it. I wish he was here – he'd be able to tell me all the constellations. If Harry and the telescope were up here then it would be Artcloud perfect. Not that Dad isn't pretty perfect, he just snores rather loudly – a bit like Grandma!

I must remember to sew a night sky hexagon, with stars. I think I really am going to try to finish the quilt for Harry. If the Guides could make their quilt in prison, I've got no excuse not to.

JULY

EXAM AND BAD HARRY MONTH

16TH JULY, DON'T ASK – IT'S ALL BAD

CLOUDS: *Cumulonimbus capillatus – the very worst storm cloud*

Dearest Diary,

I know I haven't written for ages, but here's the thing – everything has changed. Harry has been out of hospital for two weeks and I have hardly seen him. I've rung our Artcloud bell a few times, but either Joe or Lilly always come out and ask me to stop. They say Harry isn't well enough to climb trees or have visitors and they're not sure when he will be. I thought I was his best friend and almost-twin, not a freaking visitor!

This morning Grandma helped me make Harry's favourite cake. It's a chocolate toffee drizzle cake and totally delicious. We have just taken it over to Harry's house and asked if we could read him some more Changi letters. Joe went and asked him, but apparently Harry still doesn't feel like seeing "visitors".

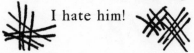 I hate him!

I saw Lilly in the kitchen, but she didn't come and say hello. Her baby bump is really big now. I hate her too. They're all trying to hide Harry away from me. What's more, Joe took the flipping cake. I asked Grandma if we could go up to Artcloud and read the rest of her Changi letters, but she said we should wait for Harry – I can't think why!

I thought Grandma might go home now Harry is out of hospital, but she says she's staying until Harry's well enough to listen to the rest of the Rosie letters and we've finished the quilt. Grandma and Mum are cooking for Joe and Lilly every night, so what with that and looking after Solo, we've not done much to the quilt lately, but it's growing slowly.

Sometimes I feel really happy to be making the quilt and imagine that when it is spread over Harry all our happy memories will work like magic to make him better. Other times I just feel cross with it and Harry and want to forget them both. Grandma told me that their Girl Guides' quilt inspired some of the women in the Changi Prison to make quilts for the men's prison. The women who thought their husbands might be in there each made a square with their initials and a message of hope. When the war finished, some of the men said that seeing those initials on the quilt was the only thing that kept them going. So I better finish our quilt, just in case it helps Harry even a little bit.

I think Harry will feel better when he has Cirrus with him. Surely he must be nearly old enough to leave his mum by now – Cirrus that is, not Harry!

P.S. I will not mention my exam results – they're rubbish. I hope Mum and Dad don't mention them either.

18TH JULY,
MY STUPID MOTHER!

CLOUDS: *None — I wish there were*

School breaks up for the summer in three days and I still haven't seen Harry since he came home. Mum keeps trying to get me to make new friends at school and hangs around the gates chatting to the other mums. How can she even think I'd ever, ever have another best friend – especially behind Harry's back. Even if I do hate him sometimes, I hate Mum more times.

Almost every day after school I go and hide in Artcloud. I've taken Edith out there for company. Occasionally someone hauls a sandwich up to me, but mostly they leave me alone. I've given up homework, I just draw cloud shapes and sew the quilt. It is almost as big as the Changi quilt now, but it has more pictures collaged on – mostly by Grandma. I miss her reading Rosie's letters, but she won't even let me see the next one until Harry is with us.

You've got to get better, Harry. I don't ever, ever, ever, ever want another best friend.

21ˢᵀ JULY,
LAST DAY OF SCHOOL

CLOUDS: *None*

Oh Diary,

There was a big end-of-term picnic in the park today. Mum collected me from school and drove me there. She had a picnic basket full of treats – even doughnuts. It was hot and my head itched. My tongue got lost and I didn't want to talk to anyone. I left Mum and ran all the way home.

Even Grandma said it was unkind of me. It was. But I just want to see my almost-twin and I don't know why I can't. Has he turned into a monster with only half a head? Maybe the surgeons chopped half of it off, like that poor boy who had his ear chopped off in Changi! I don't know. Why does nobody ever tell me what's going on? I'm not a kid any more.

22ND JULY,
FIRST DAY OF THE
SUMMER HOLIDAYS

CLOUDS: *None*

Dear Diary,

If Harry was well we'd be bouncing on the bed now celebrating six weeks of freedom from school. Well, I'm not bouncing but I am in bed. I'm staying here all day. Mum says that's fine and that she expects I'm exhausted by so much emotion.

LATER

Joe came up to see me. I told Mum not to let him in, but she did anyway. Joe says Harry has been really weak since his operation, but that he is making really good progress. Joe then said that as long as I'm just tired and don't have any germs, I can go and visit Harry tomorrow!

As soon as he'd gone I was out of bed and

bouncing my finest, highest, most bouncy bounces! I wonder if I should take the quilt to show Harry? I wonder if Grandma will come and read him another letter? I wonder if we should lend him the telescope again? Oh, I hope he's still got all his head!

23RD JULY

I saw Harry today

and my tongue

is lost

again

.

26TH JULY,
A CROSS HEDGEHOG

Dearest Diary,

I couldn't write before, but I'm all right now. It was a shock when I first saw Harry. He's just so grey and thin and very grumpy. I almost wished I hadn't gone to see him. Is that wicked?

He was lying on a giant beanbag downstairs and he made me lie beside him, but then he didn't like that and told me I should play with his Lego. Then he got really cross and told me to go away.

Lilly and Joe told me not to be upset – they said it was the medicine making Harry cross not me, so I'm trying to get used to a cross Harry. Joe and Lilly say he'll soon be on different medicine and feeling much better. I'm just going to visit for a very short time each day until then. I think it's better than not seeing him at all. At least his head is all there.

27TH JULY, QUILT EXHIBITION CLOSES

Today was the last day of the quilt exhibition, so Dad looked after Solo, and Mum, Grandma and I went to see the Changi Girl Guide quilt again. I didn't want to go without Harry, but Grandma wanted me to have one last look with her.

Now I know more about how terrible Changi was, I think it is a little patchwork miracle. There is a list of all the names of the Guides who helped to make it, and Grandma remembers every one of them. The quilt has 72 rosettes and is in a pattern called "Grandmother's Garden", which sounds just right. Grandma said that our quilt is in a pattern called "Angie's Garden". It's not. It's in a pattern called "The Almost-Twins' Garden".

AUGUST

A WONDERFUL MONTH FOR CUMULUS CLOUDS

1ST AUGUST, HOLIDAY ROUTINE

CLOUDS: *Cumulus clouds growing and shape-shifting in the sunshine*

Dearest Diary,

I've been very busy with holiday things. My hair is growing back, but my head still feels itchy. Edith is still alive. I'm keeping Artcloud clean and tidy for when Harry is well again, but I've stopped hiding in there. I see Harry most days, but some days he doesn't feel like seeing me. If I'm not working on Harry's quilt, I like to be under my bed drawing – Solo likes that too. He's a good little scribbler!

8TH AUGUST, HARRY IS BACK!

CLOUDS: *Fleets of cumulus clouds glowing in the morning sun!*

I saw Harry today and it was almost like old times. He wasn't cross and he wasn't too ghostly white. Lilly and Joe invited us all over for tea and then they asked if we would go away with them for a whole weekend!

Harry is so much better, but he is going to have to go back into hospital for a little more treatment. After that he will be really, really well. Joe and Lilly want to have a bit of a holiday before the treatment and the new baby. They even want Grandma and Solo to come! They will have little puppy Cirrus with them, so we have to stay in a dog-friendly hotel.

Which brings me to the next surprise: I am going to collect Cirrus with Harry the day after tomorrow!!! We can't wait!

Harry was allowed to come home with me after tea, which was ace. Apart from his hospital visits it was his first outing! We had to promise not to go up to Artcloud, but we went up to my bedroom. Luckily the quilt was hidden underneath my bed, because I've decided I don't want Harry to see it until it is finished.

We watched the clouds with Grandpa Jimmy's telescope until Grandma joined us and asked if we wanted her to read another Rosie letter – stupid question!

5th AUGUST, 1942

Dearest little Kitten Rosie,
More people are still arriving. We have had
to move out of our passage and into the
carpenter's shop. It is a huge room with
dozens of families all squashed in together.
Mummy, Peter and I are next to this new arrival
who is about to have her first baby. She's called
Violet and she cries a lot, because she thinks
her husband might be dead. Mummy tries to
cheer her up, but she's like a tap without a washer.

Mummy has hung our clothes from the ceiling
to make a sort of room. She also put some twigs
in an old tin and calls them her "bouquet".
I hope she's not going batty.

I've got boils all over and lumps like grapes
under my arms - they hurt. Mummy says it's
the lack of food. I hope you are not covered in
boils, my little kitten. When I get back I'll give
you six tins of sardines. I dream of food all
the time.

We've had to stop making our quilt because
we've run out of thread. We're on the hunt,
but I'm not in a hurry because sewing squashes
my boils. One of the older girls embroidered the
Girl Guides' symbol in the centre of her
rosette. It looks beautiful, but she didn't
return Mummy's sewing needle for a whole
week and she used up all our yellow thread!
She made Mummy and some of the other Guides
really angry.
Purrs and cuddles,

Girl Guide Gertie xx

I was longing to hear more, but after one short letter Harry was asleep on my bed!

THOUGHTS: I wonder if Harry will think I'm going crazy when he sees the pretend flowers I've put in Artcloud.

We won't ever run out of thread for our quilt and I've never had a boil.

Will Cirrus eat sardines?

Will my hair grow back curly or straight?

Is Harry going to get really, really, for ever better?

He has to!

10TH AUGUST,
THE BEST OF DAYS

CLOUDS: *Not one cloud in the sky!*

Woof and wag to you dear Diary,

We collected puppy Cirrus today and he is so, so gorgeous! We can't take him up into Artcloud yet because he's too wiggly and might fall out. Harry isn't allowed up there either because he's also wiggly and might fall out, so we played with snuffly, buffly, cuddly Cirrus in Harry's garden.

Cirrus already knows his name! He goes quite bonkers and runs around and around, then he suddenly goes zonk and falls fast asleep, even if he's in the middle of a game. He wees and poos everywhere so he has to stay outside, or in his crate in the kitchen. Harry's mum helped us make him a cloud bed, because Grandma and I never got around to it. When Cirrus was totally exhausted, I curled up on it with him and Harry while Grandma read us another letter. The bed is ever so cosy, but the letter was gross!

31st AUGUST, 1942

Oh Rosie,

Violet gave birth to baby Mervyn last night and it was horribly incredible! I had to help Mummy deliver him because there was nobody else. It took ages to get him out and I thought Violet might split in two!

Jimmy took care of Peter as he's too young to see such things. I won't be having children and that's for sure. You'll always be the only and most loved baby in my life, Rosie.

Strokes from Nurse Gertie xx

I just can't believe that Grandma was younger than me when she helped deliver a baby. She says she can't believe it either and wonders how she ever had children of her own after such an experience. I told Lilly then and there that I was not going to help deliver her baby! She laughed, but it's no laughing matter.

Tomorrow Harry and I are going to the pet shop to buy Cirrus some chews and treats. We have got quite a lot of money in our Artcloud money box. Cirrus was very sad when I had to go home. I know because he snuffled it into my ear!

Good news: we have decided to go away next weekend! The hotel is by the sea and we will be able to swim and eat fish and chips. Harry and I get to share a room – it is going to be so much fun! I hope the beds like being bounced on. Grandma says we can take the telescope and the rest of Rosie's letters.

I haven't done anything to Harry's quilt for ages. I've been too busy having fun with Harry and Cirrus!

11TH AUGUST, ANOTHER DAY OF CIRRUS FUN

CLOUDS: *Cumulus fractus*

Having a puppy is just the best, even if he isn't all mine. Harry is still not allowed up into Artcloud, so when Cirrus was asleep and we had a break from playing with him, Joe helped us to set up the telescope in Harry's bedroom so we can watch the clouds from there.

Harry sleeps almost as much as Cirrus and only has to look at a bed to fall asleep. I've started working on the quilt again while he rests. In the evening, Harry and I watched *Robin Hood* on television together. It's one of his favourites and he knows all the words by heart! Then Grandma read us a little, short Rosie letter, while the mums and dads planned our holiday.

8th OCTOBER, 1942

Rosie,

Such a disaster, Mummy found out that I had cut the hem off my dress! She burst into tears, because we've got no more clothes and nothing to mend clothes with. I felt sadder than if she'd been cross with me, Rosie.

I am now the only Guide who hasn't been able to find more thread for sewing my hexagons together. We are all supposed to embroider our name or a flower on our centre hexagon, but I just can't find any spare thread. I daren't take it out of my clothes seams or Mummy really will kill me! Now Miss Elizabeth may not get her quilt in time for Christmas.

Jimmy says quilting is boring and I should shut up about it. Do you think it is boring, Rosie?

Baby Mervyn is so cuddly and comes everywhere with me, but I still love you best.

Purrs and strokes from your threadless friend, Gertie

Even though it was so short, Harry was snoring by the end again. Grandma said that as time went on it got harder and harder to find paper to write letters, and in the end she ran out of paper completely. Poor Grandma.

12TH AUGUST, HIDING OUT IN ARTCLOUD ON A BLACK DAY

CLOUDS: *Cumulonimbus storm clouds*

Dear Diary and only friend,

I hate everyone except Cirrus and he's with Harry. We are not going away to the seaside. Harry saw the doctor today and she said that Harry wasn't well enough. Stupid, stupid, stupid boy! Why did he have to go and get sick? He's ruined everything – we can't even go up to Artcloud.

Lilly telephoned to ask me over, but I'm not going ever again – I'd rather hang out with the grungy girls than a boy with a sick brain! My hair's growing back and I'm glad, because Harry's is all going to fall out and it serves him right. I'm going to invite Grandma up to Artcloud and then we'll read all the Rosie letters without Harry, the rotten, hedgehog boy.

I'm never going to finish Harry's quilt. It was a rubbish idea anyway.

LATER

Grandma came up to Artcloud, but she wouldn't read Rosie's letters without Harry. She said it wouldn't be fair. Why is it always about Harry? She's gone back down now because I told her the letters were boring and the quilt was a stupid idea. Good riddance, I say. All I can see in the clouds today are roaring monsters – I think that Raiden god is eating navels again!

I've just had a look at the little bit of quilt Grandma and I have sewn together already. I think I'll keep it for myself and never give it to Harry. I'm hiding under it right now, but it's tiny and only covers my head.

What's this?

Grandma Gertie has just sent this note up to me in the pulley!

12th August,
Artcloud,
London

Dearest Angie,

You remind me so much of myself and I think I know just how you feel. When Jimmy got moved to the Changi men's prison he became very sick and I began to hate him. It was because I couldn't help him and that made me feel useless. It also meant he wasn't the tough one any more — that had to be me.

It's all right to be angry, but let's try to let in some of those "crepuscular rays" ... as Harry would say. Instead of going away, I propose an Artcloud party. What do you think? When things got bad at Changi we would arrange a party and it always made us feel better. I'll make pancakes for breakfast tomorrow if you like and we'll see if Harry will come over and make a plan.
Parents permitting, of course!

Love you, Grandma

I suppose a party might be fun, if Harry isn't sick and Cirrus doesn't poo everywhere.

P.S. I haven't forgotten that I promised never to give up on Harry, but it's not always easy – and lately it's been extremely, painfully difficult.

13TH AUGUST,
PARTY PLANNING

CLOUDS: *Contrails spread across a blue sky like rays of sunlight*

Dearest Diary,

Mum and Lilly said a party would be OK, so Harry and Cirrus came over for breakfast and we had pancakes. Harry ate six, all with chocolate spread. I ate five, three with chocolate spread and two with syrup. Cirrus ate one with a dog-treat topping!

Dad made them because Grandma was still in bed. She's full of good intentions but the early morning ones often go wrong! Anyway, it didn't matter because after breakfast we went up to her room and started our party plan.

First Grandma read us this letter where she'd written about a Changi Christmas party.

CHRISTMAS, 1942 – STILL HERE

Happy Christmas, dearest Rosie!

We had a Christmas concert today and the Guides recited a poem. The guards looked amazed by some of the clowning and magic tricks some of the prisoners performed. One guard even smiled! It was fun and some of the dads came – including my dad! We weren't allowed to talk to him, but he really was there – even Mum saw him. He was like a skeleton with just a piece of rag tied around his waist. I was bursting to hug him. The guards watched us all the time, otherwise I would have.

The Japanese commandant gave us some raisins to add to our rice and he gave every child a square of chocolate. I wish I could have shared mine with you, but maybe kittens don't like chocolate, even at Christmas. Last week the commandant gave us some palm oil but it gave everyone the runs, which was a disaster as the loos are just stinking holes in the ground!

We wished we had finished the quilt for Miss Elizabeth in time for Christmas, but we didn't manage it and we still haven't told her about it. It's partly my fault because I can't find enough thread, but the other Guides don't grumble at me. I'll be sad when the quilt is finished. It makes me happy watching it grow, and being with the other Guides. We are like a little family.

Strokes and purrs, Girl Guide Gertie

PS Jimmy says he often looks up at the clouds and imagines floating away on one. I've started doing that too. I try to catch the same cloud as Jimmy. If we ever do float away we'll be sure to come and fetch you.

I'll be sad when our quilt is finished too, because I like doing something special with Grandma. I wonder if we could finish the quilt for Harry's Christmas present?

Our party is going to have entertainment like a Changi party. The prisoners who could sing, juggle, do magic tricks, recite poetry, dance or whatever would volunteer to perform for the others. Grandma says that the Japanese guards loved watching the magic tricks. Luckily we're not entertaining any guards because none of us can do magic. Grandma remembers she and Jimmy did a juggling act at one party, but she doubts she could juggle now! We're going to have food too, which is more than the poor Changi prisoners got.

Anyway, our party is planned for tomorrow and not for Christmas, so I better get going! It has to be tomorrow because the day after Harry has to go back into hospital. If he is not allowed up into Artcloud we will put a table and chairs underneath and pretend it is a dark, stormy cumulonimbus day. Grandma is going to be in charge of food because Lilly's baby bump means she needs to rest, and Mum has Solo. Dad is doing drinks and Harry and I are in charge of entertainment. We have a plan, but it's a secret. We are going to rehearse later.

Harry suggested reading the Rosie letters as part of the entertainment, but Grandma said that they were too personal. She did agree to read us a couple more before getting up, though I think it was just an excuse to stay in bed! Anyway, we snuggled under her covers, closed our eyes and imagined...

JANUARY, 1943 – EXCITING NEWS!

Dearest Kitten Rosie,

We've finished the front of the patchwork quilt! Violet pulled the thread from the hem of her dress so that I could finish my bit – it was ever so kind of her. Now we are on the hunt for some fabric to back it all with. I hope we find it soon. I have also now earned my constellation badge and my wildflower badge!

Are you hungry, Rosie? We are. Mummy hides some of the dried rice that gets left on the sides of the cauldrons in her skirt. She gives it to the women who have a baby to feed, but it's a dangerous thing to do.

Jimmy is ten now, so he's been moved to the men's camp. His skin is covered in sun blisters and without his mummy they could get worse. I worry about him and miss him almost as much as I miss you.

I wish we could go home. I am losing count of the days and I'm running out of paper. I'll have to stop writing soon.

Purrs and strokes,
Girl Guide Gertie

JANUARY 1943

Dear Rosie,

Someone from the men's camp delivered our bag of rice today. He told Mummy that Jimmy's sun blisters have turned into ulcers and flies are laying their eggs in them - yuk, yuk, yuk! The man said he tries to help Jimmy flick the maggots out of his ulcers with bits of grass. Stupid, stupid Jimmy. We all warned him to be careful of the sun.

Mummy decided not to tell Jimmy's mummy.
Love,
Jimmy's cross friend, Gertie xxx

PS Mummy says she'll sneak us some rice sacks for the back of our quilt when the guards aren't looking! We're meant to give the empty sacks back, so she's got to be careful. The other Guides are going to be so pleased when I tell them.

It must have been terrible for Grandma when Jimmy went to the men's camp. I'm dreading Harry going back to hospital. I wish I could sit on a cloud outside his window until he's ready to come home.

After lunch we gave Cirrus a run in the garden and then Harry had to go home for a rest. I made some programmes for our party performance tomorrow. It's going to be the most brilliant party ever.

14TH AUGUST, PARTY DAY!

CLOUDS: *Not a cloud in the sky*

Dearest Diary,

It is very, very late – nearly midnight – but this has been the best day of my whole life. Better than every Christmas and birthday rolled into one – which reminds me, talking of "rolls", Harry's absolute favourite cloud is the roll cloud, only found in Australia. But I'll get him to tell you about that another time. Now I want to tell you about the party, which was fantastic.

Mum and Lilly decorated the garden with streamers, bunting, party poppers and balloons. Dad and Grandma did a mega shop and bought every food you could possibly put on your wish list! We put out cushions, rugs, hammocks, chairs, fairy lights and candles underneath Artcloud. Then at five o'clock I went and rang the Artcloud bell three times and the party began!

Solo had chosen the music (yeah right) and came dressed up as a clown, which he definitely is! Cirrus came as himself, which can't be improved on apart from his habit of stealing food and then weeing with excitement. All the grown-ups dressed in their best and drank champagne cocktails in posh glasses. Harry and I drank pretend cocktails from old jam jars.

Mum and Gertie juggled plates while dancing to Greek music, which was hilarious because every single plate smashed. Gertie was right about not being able to juggle any more! Lilly and Joe sang a very unscary ghost song and a funny song about being school girls – Joe wore a skirt and a wig! Then came the high point of the evening: the once-in-a-lifetime performance by Harry Christmas and Angela Moon.

TODAY AND TODAY ONLY

THE CLOUD NYMPH
NEPHELE
BRINGS YOU HER AMAZING AND TALENTED
CLOUD DOG CIRRUS!

*

PREPARE TO GASP WITH WONDER AS CIRRUS
JUGGLES, JUMPS THROUGH HOOPS, COUNTS
UP TO TEN, FINDS HIDDEN COINS AND BARKS
IN TIME TO NEPHELE'S TAMBOURINE!

*

TICKETS ARE FREE,
BUT A HAT WILL BE PASSED ROUND. THE AUDIENCE
ARE ENCOURAGED TO GIVE GENEROUSLY:
DOG BISCUITS, SWEETS AND MONEY
ARE ALL ACCEPTABLE.
NO FRUIT OR CUCUMBER STICKS, PLEASE — CLOUD DOGS AND NYMPHS
ARE NOT PARTIAL TO HEALTHY EATING!

*

ANGELA MOON WILL PLAY NEPHELE.
THE CLOUD DOG CIRRUS WILL BE PLAYED
BY HARRY CHRISTMAS.

Although I say it myself, it was a brilliant performance and our hat was filled to the brim. The real Cirrus barked his appreciation, especially when he found a sausage in the hat!

After the performances we ate, sang, told stories and silly jokes, and admired the stars through Grandpa Jimmy's telescope. I'm too tired to write more, but it was a great evening – the best ever.

15TH AUGUST,
PERISHING HEDGEHOG!

CLOUDS: *No clouds, just Harry!*

I was woken really early this morning by the sound of the Artcloud bell. Even in my sleep I knew this was strange. Harry isn't allowed up there and I was in my bed. Who could be ringing the bell?

Well, you guessed it, it was Harry! Not on the roof this time, but barricaded inside with Cirrus. There was a big banner outside that said: "I'M NEVER GOING BACK TO HOSPITAL AND YOU CAN'T MAKE ME!"

His mum and dad were already in the garden and they were both in tears. Harry said he would get back on the roof and jump if anyone tried to climb up to him. It was awful and I didn't know what to do so I went and got Mum and Dad. Mum took Lilly inside while Joe tried to reason with

Harry. He'd thrown all the special things I'd added to Artcloud out onto the lawn. I'd only done it to please him – he just gets harder and harder to like!

Dad wouldn't let me go up and talk to Harry because he thought I might stay up there with him, so I went and got back into bed and hid under the duvet. But that felt wrong so I watched out of the window.

It's lunchtime now and Harry's still up there. Grandma says I should try to talk him down, because he might listen to me. She says he won't get better unless he has more treatment and he knows this.

I hate him with a humungous hate, but I'm going out to try.

LATER

It was useless, I knew it would be. Harry's as stubborn as a brick.

He let Cirrus out and lowered him down in the basket, but that was it. He had the cheek to say I'd ruined Artcloud with all my "girlie stuff". Why were we ever born in the same flipping hospital? It's official, he is no longer my almost-twin. Grandma and I are going to take Cirrus and Solo to the park and I don't ever want to see Harry again. He is unfriended.

MUCH LATER

Harry is in hospital. Joe had to call an ambulance in the end, because Harry hadn't had his medicine. The ambulance people got him down. I didn't see them take him away because Grandma, Solo and I stayed out late. We had pizza, chips, dough balls and ice cream. It tasted delicious, which it probably shouldn't have done, because while Harry was having a really horrid time I was having fun.

I'm not angry now and things suddenly seem very wobbly and scary. Who will come when I ring the Artcloud bell if Harry's not there? It'll be like ringing a bell on a ghost ship – only the wind will answer.

22ND AUGUST, NO COMMENT

CLOUDS: *Cirrus*

Dear Diary,

I've had a horrible week and it probably serves me right. I should never have had that fun day out with Grandma and Solo when my almost-twin was in trouble.

Both Grandma and Harry are in hospital and everyone is snappy. Harry is not allowed visitors and Grandma didn't want any. The only good thing is that I'm looking after Cirrus full time. Also, Grandma is coming out of hospital this afternoon and Mum says she is definitely going to stay with us until her heart is stronger, which will take ages. I wish Harry could come home too – except he'd probably do something idiotic like throw himself off the roof of Artcloud. Maybe I should do something about that... Hmm, I've just had an idea – but do I dare?

Yes I do.

WATCH THIS SPACE!

23RD AUGUST,
A SMASHING NIGHT!

CLOUDS: *Not a cloud in the sky*
— not even a contrail

Well, I've done it! I crept downstairs when
everyone was asleep, took Dad's saw and
torch, unlocked the back door and climbed
up to Artcloud. I was scared out of my mind
because there were so many strange noises.
I don't know what they were, foxes maybe,
but I was shaking. I wished I had brought
Cirrus with me, but he might have barked and
woken everyone up. Anyway, I went along
to Harry's end of the walkway and started to
saw through his ladder. It took ages and made
so much noise I was sure someone would hear,
but I finally made it through and I have the
blisters to prove it. I gave the ladder a mighty
kick and it crashed to the ground. Then the
lights did go on in Harry's house and mine.

Cirrus was barking his head off and

everyone was yelling. I think they thought I was trying to saw down the whole of Artcloud! Nobody would listen to me, so I grabbed Cirrus and ran to my room and hid under the duvet. Now it's morning and I'm too scared to go downstairs. Cirrus is still curled up asleep. I've peeped out of the window – the ladder has smashed some of Joe and Lilly's plant pots. I don't care. If it stops Harry climbing up onto Artcloud and hurting himself, it's worth it.

LATER

Dearest and most patient Diary,

I'm not in too much trouble, but Dad and Mum both say that I'm to stop taking the law into my own hands. Personally, Diary, I think everyone is relieved that I've done what they didn't dare to do for fear of upsetting Harry.

Joe says I'm not to worry about the broken pots and that he'll put the ladder up again when Harry is really, really better. Mum said I had to help clear up the mess before Lilly comes back from the hospital, so that's what

I've been doing. Cirrus has been a big help. He keeps licking me – he knows what it is like to be in trouble!

SEPTEMBER

A BRAVE MONTH!

3RD SEPTEMBER, END OF THE HOLIDAYS

CLOUDS: *Cirrostratus nebulosus*

I go back to school tomorrow and Harry is still in hospital. Mum says that the doctors are worried he'll get an infection and that's why we can't visit. Lilly is never at home so she must be staying at the hospital, which means Harry isn't dead – sometimes I think nobody would tell me if he was.

I really, really, really miss him, even if he is an idiot. I'm going to go to the hospital on my own after school tomorrow. I know how to get there and I know Harry wants to see me and Cirrus. I keep thinking how much Grandma missed Jimmy when he was in the men's camp, so Harry has to see me. I've drawn a picture of Cirrus and covered it in his paw prints – I know it'll help Harry get better. I've also hidden loads of sweets, Cirrus hairs and some of Harry's cloud notebooks in my backpack – luckily I've got a big one!

Grandma is much better and we've started sewing the quilt again. Grandma is super speedy at stitching. I'm super slow, but full of amazingly brilliant ideas of what to stitch where. Grandma says at this rate our quilt will be as special as the Changi one, which is saying something!

4TH SEPTEMBER, WALKING THROUGH FOG

Dear Diary,

Did you know that fog is really a layer of low-lying stratus cloud? Probably not, but that is what it feels like in my brain this morning. Stratus translucidus is when the layer is thin enough to show the outline of the sun or moon – a little glimmer of light behind a wall of mist. I have no such glimmer.

I can't really believe I am going back to school today without Harry. I am also really frightened that when I visit Harry he won't be like the old Harry and I might wish I hadn't gone to the hospital.

Mum's calling me for breakfast – got to go.

LATER

OK, so it's like this – I did not run off to the hospital alone. Mum put a snack in my bag this morning and when she saw what was hidden in there, she guessed my plan. So Grandma took me out of school early and we went to see Harry – with the doctor's permission.

Diary, I would like to start by telling you about Harry, even though I know you know, because I've already told you. Harry is my best friend and almost-twin. We were born in the same hospital two days apart and I have been with him nearly every day of my life. If it didn't sound soppy, I would say I love him and he loves me, because we know everything the other's feeling without ever needing words. So that's enough of that, but I had to say it because I know Harry is still that Harry, but I'm frightened that the space I feel opening up may be waiting to swallow him.

I can't really write about seeing Harry. It was very quiet, but the quietness was like an extremely heavy cloud. Harry was very, very pale and didn't talk much. He was attached to all sorts of drips and wires that were connected to bleeping machines. He looked comfortable, just sleepy. Grandma put the telescope on the bed beside him. Harry must have noticed because he whispered that the telescope dated back to 1820. He was right, it does. He didn't say anything else, but Grandma decided that he must be awake so she might as well read a Rosie letter, as they are definitely one of Harry's favourite things. We didn't know if he was listening, but I held his hand, just like when we were little, and Grandma read.

But before I show you what she read, dearest Diary, I just want to say:

YOU ARE MY BESTEST,
BESTEST
FRIEND,

HARRY

CHRISTMAS!

Dearest kitten in the world,

Yesterday the worst thing ever, ever, ever happened. It was a special holiday and we were going to mix with the men's camp. We were in the exercise yard waiting and I could see Jimmy standing next to my daddy. I was so excited. Suddenly, a ripe fruit fell off a tree and split open at Jimmy's feet. He picked up a piece and ate it. A guard saw him and went mad. He said that Jimmy was a thief and started to beat him.

I don't know what happened next because we all had to go back to our rooms. I can't stop crying. Do you think they'll kill Jimmy, Rosie? I wish Jimmy hadn't done such a stupid, stupid thing. He makes me so angry - he knows any food that isn't rice, rats or bugs belongs to the Japanese.

Purrs and strokes, miserable Gertie

We were all crying by the end of the letter, even Harry, so he must have been listening. It is hard to believe that little boy was my Grandpa Jimmy. Grandma got just as cross with him as I do with that Harry Hedgehog. Yet Jimmy didn't do a thing wrong, and as for Harry – well, I just can't help wanting to murder him for being so unwell, the stupid, ridiculous, idiotic boy.

The nurse came in right at the end of Grandma's letter and was really snappy when we all started crying. Silly her, what does she know? I think crying is sometimes as good for you as laughing. Harry kept holding my hand.

I'm sorry if I've ever, ever said bad things about you, Harry. Or got cross with you when I shouldn't. I just want to finish your quilt so that you can cover yourself in all our happy memories – it'll make you feel so much better.

OCTOBER

AN EVEN BRAVER MONTH

10TH OCTOBER, JUST SADNESS

It's really hard to write, because none of us can stop thinking about Harry. He has finished his treatment and the doctors say it has gone really well, but now it's up to Harry. Harry has given up – Cirrus and I both think so. He just doesn't want to go on being ill, but I think that sometimes you've got to face up to being ill so you can get better.

The nurse at the hospital told Lilly and Joe that Grandma and I upset Harry, so they've asked us not to visit any more, which is rubbish. Seriously, Diary, it is rubbish, rubbish, rubbish. I haven't seen Harry for ages and I miss him. Mum says not to fuss Lilly, because she has enough to deal with and we don't want to bring her baby into the world too early. Flicking baby, what about Harry *leaving* the world? I can't worry about the baby too. It doesn't even have a name.

If I was Harry I'd want to be at home with my family and my new puppy. I don't think I can bring him home, but... I've just had the best idea!

11TH OCTOBER, EXHAUSTED!

Dear Diary,

WARNING: DO NOT TRY THIS.
YOU NEED SKILL AND COURAGE —
BASICALLY YOU NEED TO BE ME!

What a day! I got up so early it was only just getting light. I put Cirrus on his lead and off we set for a walk. I kept walking … and walking … and walking. Cirrus was exhausted and I had to carry him the last bit.

Eventually, we reached the hospital. Luckily by this time Cirrus was asleep in my arms and did not object to being hidden in my backpack. I walked up the steps, took the lift to Harry's floor, smiled at the duty nurse and walked straight into Harry's room. Lilly was asleep and so was Harry, so I took Cirrus out of my bag and pushed him under the blankets on the side where there were no drips or drains.

I saw Harry's hand groping around to find

what the warm bundle was. Then his eyes opened and he disappeared under the covers. Unfortunately, Cirrus was so happy to see Harry he wet the bed – but Harry laughed.

Yes, that's what I said, Harry laughed!

The next minute Lilly woke up, the nurse walked in and Cirrus fell on the floor! Then Harry burst into tears and said he wanted to go home. The nurse checked Harry's drips and drains, which luckily were all still in the right places, but she said I better leave sharpish. She picked Cirrus up and gave him a cuddle. Then instead of giving him back to me, she gave him to Harry. I was totally gobsmacked! Harry buried his head in Cirrus and told him he'd be home to look after him very soon. All I can remember after that is Lilly hugging me, and then sitting on the hospital steps with Cirrus and a security guard waiting for Dad to collect me.

I had to go to school after, which didn't seem fair, but when I finally got home Mum said she had a surprise for me. She told me to change out of my school clothes and then she took me next door. There was Harry lying on his giant beanbag, with Cirrus curled up on his stomach! Lilly gave me a hug and thanked me for being such a good and brave friend. I actually don't think I'm going to get into trouble!

Harry said that it was just like Grandma said: after the operation he felt as if he was floating on a cloud and then gradually and gently it landed him back in the world. Then when he had to go back into hospital he felt as though a stratus opacus cloud had settled over him and he couldn't see his way out and hadn't got the energy to find it. He said he had needed me and puppy Cirrus to show him the way, because his mum and dad had got lost in the cloud with him. It seems I have my uses.

Mum took me home then, because we were all exhausted. But I get to see Harry and Cirrus every day after school, and Grandma and I are going to finish the quilt extra specially quickly so that Harry has lots of happy memories to keep him well.

12TH OCTOBER, CLOUD DREAMS

Dearest Diary,

Last night I lay in bed and imagined I was on a cloud with Harry and Cirrus. It was a cumulus cloud, soft and as strong as a herd of elephants. Puppy Cirrus kept tumbling up and down its slopes. As I closed my eyes Harry became part of the cloud, pale and wispy. He was there but only just – then I fell asleep.

20TH OCTOBER, HARRY AND CIRRUS

CLOUDS: *Nimbostratus — pouring with rain*

Dearest Diary,

A lot has happened in the last few days. Best of all, I have seen Harry and Cirrus every day! Some days Harry is up and we play with Cirrus in the garden, or watch the clouds through the kitchen window. Other days he has to stay in bed and then he lies very still and hardly talks. I sit beside him and hold his hand. He likes that — although he never says. Some days Mum or Grandma come and sit with me. When Grandma comes she brings the quilt and we stitch it together. It's getting quite big now. We haven't told Harry it's for him — it'll be a surprise.

There are only three more Rosie letters left and Grandma says she is saving them for a special occasion, maybe when Harry is well enough to go up to Artcloud. I think one must be about finishing the Changi quilt, but Grandma won't say!

Grandma told us that because of the terrible conditions at Changi she'll never make old bones, which makes Harry and me laugh because Grandma couldn't be much older! She also told us that Grandpa Jimmy could only eat soup for years after they were rescued – his poor throat had closed up from lack of food. He was also plagued with skin cancer because of all that time he spent in the sun. I'd be really angry if I was Grandma, but she says anger is a waste of time. She does miss her Jimmy though. I hope I don't ever have to miss Harry.

Half term tomorrow, hooray!

26TH OCTOBER, A RAINBOW DAY

CLOUDS: *Cumulus*

Dear Diary,

You'll never guess what – Harry and I saw a rainbow today. What's special about that? Well, we saw a primary rainbow with a secondary bow that had all its colours in the reverse order. Not only that, but we also spotted "Alexander's Dark Band" in between the two rainbows – I bet we're the only cloud spotters to have noticed that.

The truth is neither Harry nor I would have seen it if Grandma hadn't pointed it out. Her Jimmy taught her how to spot the band when they were in Changi. She says a rainbow seemed like a symbol of good luck and a double rainbow, double good luck. I like the idea of double luck – with some luck for Harry and some for me, nothing can go wrong!

Grandma says it was "rainbow luck" that brought her and Jimmy back together after they left Changi. The war in the Pacific didn't end until September 1945, after the Americans had dropped two terrible atomic bombs on Japan. After that the Japanese surrendered and the prison guards handed Changi over to the Allied soldiers in the men's camp. Grandma says there were rumours that the guards were going to kill everyone before they surrendered, but they didn't. Anyway, eventually all the prisoners were put on hospital ships and sent to England or Australia. Grandma's family went back to England and she lost touch with Jimmy. She thought she would never see him again.

When Grandma's family had recovered, Grandma's father was sent back to Singapore. Grandma finished her schooling there and then started to train as a nurse. One rainy, rainbow day while she was a student nurse, who should she find on her ward but Jimmy! After that Grandma and Jimmy were never parted again. Grandma says she doesn't think either of them could have married someone who hadn't been in Changi, because it left them with so many awful memories as well as health problems.

Jimmy told Grandma that before he left Changi he had gone to look for his telescope. He hardly dared believe he'd find it, but there it was still in its hiding place, along with Grandma's letters to Rosie. So when Gertie was reunited with Jimmy, she was also reunited with her letters. After that the letters and the telescope always stayed together, just like Jimmy and Grandma.

I will be so sad when Jimmy sends a cloud for his Gertie, but I can feel that she longs to be with him again. Just not quite yet – please, Grandma.

No Grandma, we need you here and you haven't read all the Rosie letters yet.

Hey, who said you could write in my diary?

Cirrus!

NOVEMBER

COLD, RAINY
AND BLEAK

1ST NOVEMBER

CLOUDS: *Nimbostratus*

I haven't done much jotting recently on
account of Harry. He's not been very lively so
I've been keeping him company and looking
after Cirrus. Harry doesn't talk much at the
moment, he just lies on his beanbag listening
to my bad jokes. Even when his head hurts
really badly, which it sometimes does, I can
make him smile. It's lucky my dad is such
a clown, or I wouldn't know so many
rubbish jokes!

Harry's baby brother or sister is due in two and a half weeks – what will it be? Harry wants a little sister. I think it would be nice if it was a little boy for Solo to play with – but then, as you may have noticed, I quite like boys!

LATER – EMERGENCY!

Would you believe it, I had just written the above when Lilly was rushed into hospital to have the baby, ten days early!

It's a girl called Fleur, which is French for flower. Harry chose the name after seeing the flowers on the Changi quilt! Grandma was dead chuffed and says we will now have to put the same flowers on Harry's quilt which, by the way, is still growing.

Lilly has to stay in hospital for a bit, because Fleur was early, so I am going to stay with Harry, Cirrus and Joe, just to keep them company. A funny, bubbly nurse comes to make sure Harry has the right medicine, because Joe is a bit rubbish at that sort of thing. But he is an ace artist. He drew a picture of baby Fleur for us, because we are not going to see her until she comes home, which might not be for a few days. Joe and I also drew lots of pictures of dogs and cloud nymphs and stuck them all over the walls for Harry to look at.

FACT: It's going to be fun staying with Harry and Joe. I don't even mind when Harry is cross with me, because it's only when his head hurts. Joe lets us eat crisps and watch as much telly as we want. Actually, it's wicked nobody ever says no to Harry now, so we get to eat and drink whatever we want. If I feel like a fizzy drink and a bowl of sweets, I just say Harry wants them and hey presto – they appear like magic!

CANINE FACT: Cirrus never leaves Harry's beanbag, except to eat or have a run in the garden with me. Even then he rushes back to Harry, licks his face and snuggles under the blanket beside him. I think Cirrus is trying to help Harry get better by giving him lots and lots of love and magic licking.

SECRET: They'll be snuggling under Harry's quilt soon, because we're going to give it to him for Christmas. And unlike those Changi Girl Guides, we will get our quilt finished in time!

2ND NOVEMBER,
ANOTHER LETTER

CLOUDS: *Altocumulus*

Grandma and Mum came over this evening
and we all had supper together. Grandma said
the birth of Fleur yesterday made it a special
enough day to read another letter. As there
are only three left we are eking them out
and hoping the quilt gets finished before
the letters!

15th MARCH, 1943
THE CARPENTER'S SHOP, CHANGI

Dearest and best cat Rosie,

We've had a horrid time since Jimmy was beaten. He nearly died and was in hospital for ages, but Doctor Lake says he's nearly better. The guards haven't stopped shouting at us and we're totally banned from gathering in groups now. Most of the Guides meet anyway, but someone always keeps watch. Even so, we've almost finished the quilt! It took Mummy ages to collect enough rice sacks. She got caught taking one, but pretended it was Baby Mervyn's dirty nappy. Not even the guards wanted to check that! Now we have to unpick the sacks, wash them and sew them to the hexagons.

Hugs and purrs, your stick-thin friend, Gertie

Harry and I felt so proud of Grandma and the other Guides. They just never gave up, however dangerous it was. I think my great-great-grandma was pretty amazing too – imagine tricking the guards like that!

I can't wait to hear the rest of the letters.

3RD NOVEMBER, A CREPUSCULAR BABY FLEUR DAY!

CLOUDS: *Cirrostratus*

I got to have the day off school to celebrate the birth of Fleur! She came home today and Harry, Joe and I got all dressed up to welcome her. Harry dressed as the cloud dog Cirrus, but was then sick all down the clouds and had to become a boy on a beanbag. I was Nephele the cloud nymph. Cirrus WAS Cirrus, but with a blue bow, and Joe wore a pirate's outfit without the eye patch, because we thought that might scare Fleur! We made Fleur and Lilly a cake covered in pink icing. I tried to write Fleur's name on it, but it went sort of wonky.

LATER

I am back home now. You can have too much of all that baby mush. Even sane adults and boys cry, gurgle and coo when they see a new baby. Harry let Fleur lie beside him and Cirrus on the beanbag and they all fell asleep together. Lilly thought it was "so sweet" – I thought it was soppy. You would never know they are brother and sister – Harry is very pale and his hair is still blond with curly wisps, while Fleur is very pink and has loads of dark straight hair. I'm much more like Harry than Fleur is.

I wonder if Fleur and Solo will be best friends like Harry and me.

5TH NOVEMBER

CLOUDS: *A cumulonimbus thundercloud day*

Dear Diary,

Everything is rubbish: school is rubbish, home is rubbish, Artcloud is rubbish, clouds are rubbish and even drawing is rubbish. I can't write what's wrong, because it is worse than rubbish and there aren't words for it. It's Harry's and my very best day of the year. We always have a firework party and watch the rockets light up the night clouds. We could have watched them from Artcloud this year – except we didn't. I don't understand why because even if you're not well you can still enjoy watching the sky light up.

I hate everyone and everything and I don't ever want to see Harry again. I should never, ever have been friends with him. I knew I shouldn't have been, he's a boy, a stupid, stupid, stupid boy.

15TH NOVEMBER, MY BESTEST FRIEND EVER, EVER, EVER!

I don't know what to write and I don't do cloud spotting any more.

Harry has given up the beanbag and taken to his mum and dad's bed. He is like a little pale prince, lying in a white fairytale bed. He is my bestest, bestest friend and I know I am his. Sometimes he makes everyone go away except his mum, Cirrus and me. He always smiles at me and we mostly just hold hands. Sometimes, he wants to watch me draw clouds, and I sit beside him on the bed and draw little clouds with funny faces. Other times I just lie on the bed beside him and tell him about the clouds I pretend to see on the ceiling, what shapes they make and their names, because Harry's eyes are too blurry to see many clouds any more. It's like we're in Artcloud together, except we aren't. I can't do jokes any more, I can't seem to remember them.

When the nurse comes she tries to send me away, but that makes Harry cross and his head hurt.

Sometimes Harry likes Fleur to lie beside him too. Lilly and Joe don't have family close by so Mum and Grandma are trying to help by cooking for them and looking after little Fleur.

25TH NOVEMBER, ONE MONTH UNTIL CHRISTMAS!

Only one month until Christmas – I'd forgotten about it until today. I rushed around and banged on Harry's door. Amazingly, he was downstairs watching telly, so I reminded him of his promise. Even though he can't talk at the moment, he PROMISED to be well for Christmas, he really did and you NEVER, NEVER break a promise. Harry held my hand really tight and pretended to pull a cracker. He will be better – I know he will.

I told Lilly about the promise and she told Harry about the Christmas cake she's planning to make. It's going to be blue with white clouds floating around it, and hidden in the clouds will be Christmas robins with flowers in their beaks for Fleur and drawing pens for me.

Lilly said everyone would sing "I Wish I Were a Christmas Cloud" as well as "Happy

Christmas", and she'd heard that Father Christmas had a whole extra sack of presents loaded onto his sleigh just for Harry and me! Not that Harry and I believe in Father Christmas, but we carry on pretending for our parents.

Anyway, it will be the best Christmas ever, I know it will. I've made Harry and me a chart so we can cross off the days until then.

Grandma and I were having a blitz on Harry's quilt, but then Grandma said that she thought it was a time to make memories and not to save them, so why didn't we just spend a bit of time doing special things and visiting Harry. Well, it is a busy time so she may have a point, but I do, do, do want to finish the quilt by Christmas.

DECEMBER

CHRISTMAS IS COMING!

15TH DECEMBER, END OF TERM

The last day of term today, hooray! When I got home I changed and went straight over to Harry's. He did seem a lot better. When I whispered that it was only ten more days to Christmas, he wiggled a finger and Cirrus wagged his tail.

I sat and held Harry's hand. I didn't move because I think it hurts his head if I wriggle. Lilly says that Harry can hear us, even if he doesn't answer. I wish he would answer – just a hedgehog snuffle would do.

Then Mum came over to return Fleur and get me for supper. I didn't want to leave.

If Harry could still write, he might write: Good night, stinky Knickers!

23ᴿᴰ DECEMBER, CIRRUS WALKING

Dear Diary,

I took Cirrus for a long walk in the park with Dad, Mum and Solo. Mum tried to talk to me about Harry not getting better, but I ran away with Cirrus. There's things you know inside but don't want to hear, and that's one of them.

Besides, I have other things on my mind: it's nearly Christmas and I've got a plan for Harry's second present, since Grandma thinks we might not finish the quilt.

It is going to be wicked. It looks like a cloud on a stick, but when you push the stick up the cloud dog Cirrus appears – it's sure to make Harry laugh.

Dad is going to find me the bits so I can make it tomorrow and Grandma is muttering about reading us the last two Rosie letters as a pre-Christmas treat.

Maybe she'll even finish Harry's quilt –

although I can hear her saying "There's a time for being and a time for doing"!

CHRISTMAS EVE

Lilly and Joe had friends and family round so I didn't visit Harry in the day. Then in the evening Joe came to say Harry was asking for me. I went over to tell Harry that I was busy making his Christmas present, so I hoped he had something important to say – not that he can talk any more, but his mum can understand him and I can too sometimes.

Anyway, he wants me to have his stuffed owl for a Christmas present, and everything else of his in Artcloud. Stupid hedgehog boy – what will I do with his daft owl? It hasn't even got any sweets left in it. And as for his books on clouds, his cloud blanket, cloud cushion and crazy cloud notebooks – he's gone flipping bonkers if he thinks I want them.

Harry held on to my hand, but I had to go and finish his present. At least it's new and not some idiot boy's leftovers. This is going to be the worst Christmas ever.

It's really late now. I've finished and wrapped Harry's present. Mum has hung my stocking up for Father Christmas. I didn't do it, because I don't feel ready for Christmas. It should be next week or even next year, but not tomorrow. Besides, Grandma and I haven't finished Harry's quilt yet.

I don't even want to know what happens next 'cos it's a rubbish Christmas already.

CHRISTMAS DAY

CLOUDS: *Altostratus — it could snow!*

Well, I did have the best Christmas ever, ever, ever!

I had a ginormous stocking full of everything I could possibly ever want for painting, drawing, scribbling, sticking, sewing and writing. My mum is the best "Father" Christmas and Dad cooks the best Christmas breakfast of waffles with lashings of maple syrup. Grandma had such a big present for me she couldn't carry it downstairs – she had to put it on a tray and slide it down! When I opened it there was nothing in it – ho ho ho! Then tucked in the bottom I found the box with Grandpa Jimmy's telescope. The card with it said: **To Angie and Harry, the bestest of friends.** I was bursting to tell Harry that we could keep the telescope for ever and ever.

At lunchtime we all went over and knocked on Harry's door and Joe answered it with Harry on his back – just like old times! Harry was dressed in his favourite Cirrus the cloud dog onesie, with slippers like dog paws and sunglasses. We had a picnic Christmas lunch on beanbags and little picnic tables. It was the biggest, most nutty, sprouty, crackery, joke-filled lunch ever. For pudding we had Lilly's Christmas cake with ice cream. The cake was brilliant and it was covered with candles which Harry and I blew out together – except I did most of the blowing. Everyone sang cloud songs, told cloud jokes, pulled cloud crackers and ate more cake, more ice cream, more chocolates and more sweets. Cirrus barked, Fleur cried, Solo clapped and everyone had fun, especially Harry and me.

Then, just as we had collapsed around the Christmas tree, there was a knock at the door. "Ho, ho, ho!" It was Joe dressed up as Father Christmas and Lilly and Fleur dressed as his elf helpers! They handed out the presents and I'm certain that Harry liked my cloud on a stick best. I'm sure it reminded him of all our jumping up and down on beds, cloud spotting and dog loving!

When Mum and Dad took Solo home to bed, Lilly asked if Grandma and I would like to stay and watch a film with Harry. Well, she didn't actually ask Grandma, because Grandma was asleep and snoring on her beanbag. So Harry and I watched *The Jungle Book*, which is one of Harry's favourites. Then guess what? Grandma woke up and said she thought I should get Harry's quilt and show it to him, even though it's not quite finished.

So I did. I pointed out every memory to Harry: the bouncing, Artcloud, Cirrus, Miss Lemonpops, sweets, owls, hedgehogs, clouds, stars, cucumber sticks, doughnuts with sprinkles, the telescope, the almost-twins ... and Harry smiled and smiled. Then we curled up together on his beanbag and Grandma hid us under the quilt, while she read us the last two Rosie letters.

Rosie,

We finished the quilt! It looks so wonderful. Miss Elizabeth was thrilled. I don't think she could believe her eyes. She said it was the most beautiful, colourful thing inside the whole of Changi Prison and filled her with hope. I'll miss making it and being with my Guide family, even though the guards were always giving us frights. One day I'll make you something beautiful, Rosie.

Purrs and strokes, quilt-maker Gertie.

Isn't that amazing? The Guides actually managed to finish the quilt! In spite of everything, they just kept going until they had made it. As Harry and I hid under our quilt, we were totally in awe.

There was just one more letter left. I asked Grandma if we could read it another day, because I thought Harry might be falling asleep. But Grandma said she thought it best to keep reading, and so she did.

APRIL, 1943
CHANGI PRISON - STILL UNRESCUED

Dearest Kitten Rosie,

This might be my last letter - I'm just so scared. The guards found a radio in the men's camp and now they are searching everywhere! What if they find Jimmy's you-know-what? All your letters are hidden and I daren't go near them. I will try to post them one day.

We are all starving and eating leaves and insects. I thought of you when I tried to catch a rat to eat. I didn't get it, thank goodness.

Goodbye, dearest Rosie, I miss you and Jimmy so much. Sardines, purrs and strokes,

Hungry, hungry, hungry Gertie

PS Did I tell you that the Guides started a quilting craze? All the women are making them now - but ours came first!

It felt so sad that this was the last of the letters. I wished Grandma had saved it so that Harry and I still had it to look forward to. I expect Grandma felt that about finishing the quilt – you want to finish, but then again you don't. At least Grandma knew the Guides had inspired the women to make quilts – and now she has inspired me to make a quilt too! Even if it wasn't finished for Christmas, it did feel quite special and magical as Harry and I lay underneath our memories.

I think Grandma felt extra sad after reading the last letter, because she had tears on her cheek. Maybe it made her miss Jimmy more than ever. I hope not.

I must have fallen asleep beside Harry. I sort of remember Dad carrying me home and now it's morning and I've just woken up in my own bed – still in my Christmas clothes and wrapped in Harry's quilt.

THANK YOU EVERYONE, FOR A BRILLIANT CHRISTMAS!

BLACK BOXING DAY

I wanted to rush outside and ring the Artcloud bell so Harry and I could talk about our amazing Christmas. Then I remembered that he wouldn't, couldn't, probably not ever again come up to Artcloud. It was like my stomach was weighed down by a ton of blackness.

Well, I thought, I can still go and talk to Harry. Only Mum said I should wait a bit because he might be tired after so much Christmas fun, so I hid under my bed.

LATER

Joe came round and sat on my bed. He asked me if I wanted to sit with Harry for a bit. He said Harry was asleep and might not wake up, but he would know I was there. Joe said Harry had been very brave and had waited to share Christmas with us, but now he was ready to leave us for a new adventure.

I didn't want to go and see Harry. I wanted to stay under my bed.

Mum came up and lay down beside me.

We didn't talk, we just held hands. It made me want to hold Harry's hand, because he liked me to do that. Harry wouldn't want to go on a new adventure without a hand to hold – so Mum and I went next door together.

Harry was asleep in his big white bed, breathing like a rattle, the silly hedgehog. His mum and dad were beside him and Cirrus too. I snuggled in among them and hugged my bestest ever friend and held his little hand.

I don't remember much more. I think Dad came and carried me home. The thing I do remember and always will is that Harry died this very night. I will always, always remember that, even though I'll never see that stupid, stupid, idiot boy again.

I love you Harry Christmas.
You'll always be my bestest friend
and almost-twin.

27TH DECEMBER

I'M NOT TALKING AND I'M NOT
WRITING EVER, EVER AGAIN.

IT'S ALL SO STUPID AND I KNOW IT IS MY
OWN FAULT FOR BEING FRIENDS WITH A BOY.
I NEVER, **EVER** SHOULD HAVE.

I DON'T CARE ANY MORE,
REALLY I DON'T.

I HATE **EVERYBODY** AND **EVERYTHING**

AND I *ESPECIALLY* HATE THOSE
STUPID CLOUDS THAT KEEP ON
MOVING THE SKY AROUND.

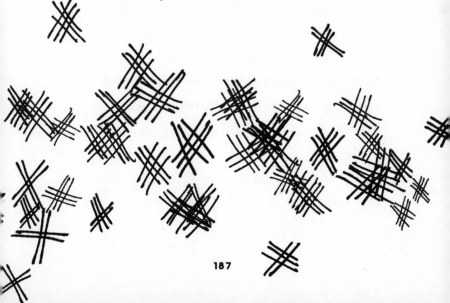

JANUARY

1ST JANUARY, HARRY'S CELEBRATION DAY

There is a special party at Harry's house today to celebrate his life. Lilly has made all his favourite foods. Everyone has been very kind to me, like I'm ill or something. Joe made a speech and thanked me for being Harry's friend. Now I've come up to Artcloud to hide, because my tongue has run away and I can't talk to people. I don't even know what to say. I should have said something about Harry being my almost-twin, but it's too secret.

There is a bouncy castle for the children to bounce on. I can see kids playing on it through my spy hole. Harry did love to bounce, but just looking at it makes me cry. I can't stop crying now.

Last night I woke up and thought Harry was bouncing on my bed. Then I thought I heard the Artcloud bell ring, but it must have been my imagination because Harry's not here any more. But still I hear the bell and see the covers on my bed move up and down, up and down, up and down.

Maybe one day Harry will send me a message in the clouds. I think he will. I hope it says: "My head doesn't hurt now and I haven't turned into a hedgehog!"

I have just been out onto the walkway and sung "How Sweet to be a Cloud" as loudly as I could into the night. I expect Harry heard it.

3RD JANUARY, NO HARRY

It's worse than you can ever imagine and it won't ever, ever get better. I'm supposed to go back to school next week, but I'm going to hide in Artcloud for ever and ever. If I keep looking I might see Harry on a cloud. I'm frightened I will, and I'm frightened I won't.

If I could talk to Harry just once more I think I might feel better. I could tell him a cloud joke and make him smile.

4TH JANUARY
I HATE SCISSORS.
HARRY SHOULDN'T HAVE LEFT THEM BEHIND.

Things just get worse and worse and all because of Harry. I've done a terrible thing and everyone hates me, but I don't care. It's all the fault of that stupid, stupid, rubbish boy. I hate him – he just makes me SO angry. Would I ever have gone and died on him? Not a chance in hell!

I was lying in Artcloud looking up through the window to see if there was a message for me in the clouds, but there weren't any clouds and there wasn't any Harry. He was always messing me about and pretending not to be there when he was, and now he's still doing it. He made me so mad that I took his scissors and cut up all his cloud notebooks, his horrid cloud blanket, his ridiculous cloud cushion and his stupid owl. Everything is in bits and covered in cushion feathers and I'm glad, really, really glad.

Only somehow Lilly found out and she won't stop crying. She's still standing halfway up Harry's ladder saying, "How could you, how could you?" Mum is there too and she's also crying, so now I've barricaded the door and I'm going to stay here for ever and cut up everything, even the cloud pictures I did for Harry.

I wish they would all go away and leave me alone.

GO AWAY!

LATER

I think I've been asleep. It's freezing cold and very dark outside.

I am all alone now, Mum and Lilly aren't outside.

5TH JANUARY

Dad broke in to Artcloud in the night with hot chocolate and blankets. We didn't speak, but we slept curled up together and it felt much warmer.

It's morning now and I've been inside for breakfast, but I'm not really hungry so I've come back out to Artcloud. I wish I hadn't been angry and cut everything up – it won't ever go back together and there are feathers everywhere. It wasn't Harry's fault, I know it wasn't and now everything of his is gone and I should have kept it all just perfect, the way he liked it. I don't think Lilly will ever talk to me again or let me play with Cirrus, even though Harry said he was my dog too.

6TH JANUARY

I've moved back into the house because it's so cold in Artcloud.

Grandma Gertie isn't angry with me and nor is Solo. Solo just giggles all the time. I think he really likes me, even with my spiky new hair.

BAD: Lilly is very, very upset and doesn't want to see me. She, Joe and Fleur have gone to stay with friends, and they've taken Cirrus. It's my fault – those were Harry's things and I shouldn't have chopped them up even if he had given them to me. I wish I hadn't. Mum says I should write to Lilly and say how sorry I am. She says Lilly and Joe are very, very sad right now and sometimes sadness can make you angry – as if I didn't know that. It's all right for adults, they're allowed to be cross but kids aren't – even if their hearts are aching fit to split in two and they're covered by a great black cloud.

GOOD: I am not going back to school next week.

Mum has told them I'll go back the week after.

BAD: I think Harry would be very unhappy that I made his mum cry when she is already so sad. Oh Harry, I am so, so sorry.

What can I do to make it better, Harry?

ANSWER ME, YOU FLICKING HEDGEHOG!

7TH JANUARY,
NO SCISSORS NEEDED!

I've had an idea. It won't mend Harry's things, but I think he will like it just the same. Grandma is going to look after Solo while Mum takes me shopping.

LATER

It's done and it made Mum and me happy and sad at the same time. We bought ten helium balloons in all that hedgehog's favourite colours. I tied them together with a secret message and a bag of his favourite sweets. We walked to the top of Park Hill and I ran and ran until just the right moment, then I let go of the balloons and they flew up high into the clouds. Higher and higher they went, through the cirrus clouds and up to where the clouds are as strong as a herd of elephants, strong enough to hold Harry, so I hope he's sucking on those sweets right now.

One day I might be a glider pilot, then I

can fly up there myself and drop things off to Harry – maybe even have a chat.

I wanted to phone Joe and Lilly and tell them what I'd done, but Mum and Dad say I must wait until they are less upset. I wish they'd let me walk Cirrus. Apart from Harry he's my best friend.

8TH JANUARY, THAT'S GRANDMA FOR YOU!

CLOUDS: *Cumulus*

When I got up this morning Grandma Gertie was already sitting at the kitchen table cutting out yet more cardboard squares and hexagons. It is her turn to have a brilliant idea and it's just the best.

Grandma and I are going to use the chopped-up bits of Harry's stuff to finish his quilt. We can even sew in some of the feathers, and have bits of his notebooks copied onto fabric! Grandma says she knew there was some reason why we hadn't finished his quilt in time for Christmas, but she never suspected it was because I was going to go on a chopping frenzy! So now my quilt, which is really Harry's, will have even more memories in it and will always remind me of the most amazing friend ever. Even when

I'm old and grey and my memory is slipping, I will be able to point at the patches and tell my grandchildren, and great-grand-children, about the adventures that Harry and I had together. Maybe I should make Fleur a little quilt too, so she knows what an amazing crepuscular brother she had – I think I might!

I have so many memories of things me and Harry shared together. Grandma says it makes her dizzy just to think about all those hexagons and squares! But, just like the Changi quilt, we will finish it and it will be a very happy quilt! Some of the most special hexagons will be Grandma Gertie sharing her memories of Changi with us, and I'm going to embroider a picture of little Kitten Rosie as a surprise for her.

Did I ever tell you, Diary, that Grandma did find out what had happened to Kitten Rosie, even though she never saw her again? So much has happened, sometimes I can't remember what I've written about and what's left out. She told Harry and me that after the war, her old nanny sent her a letter and a photograph of Rosie. When the Japanese took over Singapore, Gertie's nanny escaped to a village with Rosie, who had eventually grown into a very large cat! Grandma thinks she lived like a princess on sardines and champagne. I'll have to put those in the quilt too!

Grandma says that much of our sadness will get caught up and carried away by our stitching. I doubt that, but she's the quilting queen so she may be right. I'm off to Artcloud now to collect together all the bits that I chopped up – I knew I'd done it for a reason!

Well, Diary, I think I'll say goodbye for now because I'm going to be tied up in thread for the next few weeks and, as you know, I'm not really a writing sort of person!

P.S. Solo says my name now – well, I think he does. Mind you, when I used to take him over to see Harry they would make rude noises together, so it might just be one of those!

Solo is quite clever though – he is already trying to walk.

P.P.S. When I woke up this morning I saw the sunlight shining through the window like speckled gold. I managed to capture some of it in a jar, and when I'm older I'll go up in a glider and sprinkle it out of the cockpit to make a sunbeam quilt to keep Harry warm on cold, dark days, just as his quilt will keep me warm.

P.P.P.S. You won't believe this, but I saw a Kelvin-Helmholtz cloud today – just for a second, then it curled in on itself and vanished. It was stunning. I bet that stupid hedgehog boy saw it too.

I may never see you again, Harry, but you'll always mean the world to me. Goodbye Harry Hedgehog, my almost-twin.

THE END

ONE LAST THING

When I went to collect all the bits I'd chopped up, I found this note of Harry's:

THE MORNING GLORY: a roll cloud formed by stratocumulus clouds.
This cloud is the most amazing cloud in the whole wide world. It only appears in a remote part of Australia and can stretch up to six hundred miles long.
In September and October glider pilots hang around hoping it will form so that they can take their gliders up and "surf the cloud"! One day Angie and I will surf the Morning Glory, but we'll have to become glider pilots first!

One day I will become a glider pilot and surf the Morning Glory. And when I do I'll take this note and a picture of Harry with me, because it wouldn't be the same surfing the Morning Glory without my almost-twin and bestest friend.

NIMBOSTRATUS OR ALTOSTRATUS OPACUS

STRATOCUMULUS NON-CUMULOGENITUS

STRATOCUMULUS CUMULOGENITUS

CUMULUS HUMILIS OR FRACTUS

CUMULUS & STRATOCUMULUS

ALTOCUMULUS TRANSLUCIDUS (IN BANDS)

ALTOCUMULUS OPACUS OR DUPLICATUS

ALTOCUMULUS CUMULOGENITUS

ALTOCUMULUS CASTELLANUS OR FLOCCUS

ALTOCUMULUS OF A CHAOTIC SKY

CIRROSTRATUS

CIRROSTRATUS

CIRROCUMULUS

STRATUS FRACTUS

CUMULUS FRACTUS

CUMULUS & STRATOCUMULUS

CUMULUS CONGESTUS OR MEDIOCRIS

CUMULONIMBUS CALVUS

CUMULONIMBUS CAPILLATUS

ALTOCUMULUS TRANSLUCIDUS

ALTOCUMULUS OF A CHAOTIC SKY

CIRRUS FIBRATUS

CIRRUS SPISSATUS

CIRRUS SPISSATUS CUMULONIMBOGENITUS

CIRRUS FIBRATUS OR UNCINUS

STRATUS FRACTUS

CUMULUS FRACTUS

ALTOSTRATUS TRANSLUCIDUS

NIMBOSTRATUS OR ALTOSTRATUS OPACUS

STRATOCUMULUS NON-CUMULOGENITUS

CUMULONIMBUS CAPILLATUS

ALTOCUMULUS TRANSLUCIDUS

PATCHES OF ALTOCUMULUS TRANSLUCIDUS

ALTOCUMULUS TRANSLUCIDUS (IN BANDS)

ALTOCUMULUS CUMULOGENITUS

CUMULUS HUMILIS OR FRACTUS

CUMULUS & STRATOCUMULUS

CUMULUS CONGESTUS OR MEDIOCRIS

CUMULONIMBUS CALVUS

CUMULONIMBUS CAPILLATUS

ALTOCUMULUS CASTELLANUS OR FLOCCUS

ALTOCUMULUS OF A CHAOTIC SKY

CIRRUS FIBRATUS

CIRRUS SPISSATUS

CIRRUS SPISSATUS CUMULONIMBOGENITUS

CUMULUS CONGESTUS OR MEDIOCRIS

CUMULONIMBUS CALVUS

CUMULONIMBUS CAPILLATUS

ALTOCUMULUS TRANSLUCIDUS

PATCHES OF ALTOCUMULUS TRANSLUCIDUS

CIRRUS FIBRATUS

CIRRUS SPISSATUS

CIRRUS SPISSATUS CUMULONIMBOGENITUS

CIRRUS FIBRATUS OR UNCINUS

CIRRUS & CIRROSTRATUS

CIRRUS & CIRROSTRATUS

ALTOSTRATUS TRANSLUCIDUS

NIMBOSTRATUS OR ALTOSTRATUS OPACUS

STRATOCUMULUS NON-CUMULOGENITUS

STRATOCUMULUS CUMULOGENITUS

CUMULUS HUMILIS OR FRACTUS

PATCHES OF ALTOCUMULUS TRANSLUCIDUS

ALTOCUMULUS TRANSLUCIDUS (IN BANDS)

ALTOCUMULUS OPACUS OR DUPLICATUS

ALTOCUMULUS CUMULOGENITUS

ALTOCUMULUS CASTELLANUS OR FLOCCUS

CIRRUS & CIRROSTRATUS

CIRRUS & CIRROSTRATUS

CIRROSTRATUS

CIRROSTRATUS

CIRROCUMULUS

STRATOCUMULUS CUMULOGENITUS

CUMULUS HUMILIS OR FRACTUS

CUMULUS & STRATOCUMULUS

CUMULUS CONGESTUS OR MEDIOCRIS

CUMULONIMBUS CALVUS

ALTOCUMULUS CASTELLANUS OR FLOCCUS

ALTOSTRATUS TRANSLUCIDUS

NIMBOSTRATUS OR ALTOSTRATUS OPACUS

STRATOCUMULUS NON-CUMULOGENITUS

STRATOCUMULUS CUMULOGENITUS

ALTOCUMULUS TRANSLUCIDUS

PATCHES OF ALTOCUMULUS TRANSLUCIDUS

ALTOCUMULUS TRANSLUCIDUS (IN BANDS)

ALTOCUMULUS OPACUS OR DUPLICATUS

ALTOCUMULUS CUMULOGENITUS

CIRRUS FIBRATUS OR UNCINUS

CIRRUS & CIRROSTRATUS

CIRRUS & CIRROSTRATUS

CIRROSTRATUS

CIRROSTRATUS

ABOUT THIS BOOK

In February 1942, Olga Morris was living with her family in Singapore when it was captured by the Japanese. Along with 2,400 other civilians, Olga, her mother and her sister were incarcerated in Changi Prison – a jail built to house just 600 prisoners. The conditions were appalling, with families crammed together in tiny cells measuring eight foot by six foot, with one concrete bed, rats and an endless diet of rice.

But once everyone had settled in, one of the main problems became boredom, particularly among the children. So in 1943 Elizabeth Ennis, who had been a nurse in the Indian Army before being captured, set up a Girl Guide group that met once a week. Olga, along with nineteen other girls aged between eight and sixteen years, joined the group and they quickly bonded into a close unit with Mrs Ennis as their much-loved Guide leader.

The Guides would meet in the corner of the exercise yard, where Olga remembers saying the Guide Promise and singing songs. Luckily, along with the seven dresses Olga's mother had worn for the long, hot walk to the prison, she had also hidden some needles and thread about her person, so the Guides were able to embroider their badges.

Faced with the horrors of living under the watchful eyes of the Japanese guards, and the lack of food and sanitation, the group gave the children a sense of hope and community. To thank Mrs Ennis, they decided to secretly make her a little coverlet of hexagons. They had no idea how long it would take, or if they would ever be able to finish it, but they decided to start it anyway.

The supply of thread that Mrs Morris had brought into the jail quickly ran out, so the girls began to unpick the seams of clothes that had rotted from repeated wear under the sun. The fabric for the hexagons was cut from the same rotten dresses, or snipped from the hems of dresses still being worn. The Guides found a little cell where they met in secret to stitch the quilt. The guards hated groups to gather, even if they were made up of young children, so if the girls heard a guard approaching they would stuff their sewing into their knickers for fear of being punished. Eventually they managed to finish the quilt and found enough rice sacks to make a backing. One can hardly imagine how overwhelmed Mrs Ennis must have been to receive something so charming and full of hope, born out of the grim misery of internment.

This beautiful little quilt became an inspiration for the women in Changi Prison. They made quilts for the men's camp, with stitched coded messages so that their husbands and loved ones would know that they were still alive and thinking of them. Three quilts were eventually made. The first one was made to appease the guards, with the flag and flowers of Japan. Then two more were made and embroidered for the men's camp. Until the men saw the quilts, many of them had no idea if their wives and daughters were still alive. On one of the quilts, Mrs Ennis embroidered an ocean liner with a banner saying "Homeward Bound" and then signed it. When this quilt was delivered by the Red Cross to the men's camp, Mr Ennis could hardly believe that his wife was still alive. He said later that this little message kept him going for the remainder of his internment.

I first saw the Changi Guide quilt in 2010, when it was in an exhibition at the V&A Museum. I was immediately struck by how, after so many years, this quilt is still a powerful symbol of young people's love and endurance. I was later introduced to Olga (now Olga Henderson), the only surviving Guide from Changi Prison, and she generously shared her memories with me. Grandma Gertie's letters are based on Olga's story. Although, with Olga's kind permission, I have taken liberties here and there so that I could create my own patchwork quilt by stitching together Gertie's story with Harry and Angie's. This may seem an odd choice of design, but for me both stories tell of the immense courage, loyalty and love shown by young people in the direst of circumstances. They are, for me, a symbol of hope – I trust they will be for you.

Marcia Wiliams, 2018

ABOUT THE AUTHOR

MARCIA WILLIAMS was born in England but spent her childhood in Hong Kong, Cyprus, Nigeria and at Swiss and English boarding schools. After she left school Marcia kicked around for a few years, got married, had a family, did an MA in Children's Literature and then finally settled down to writing and illustrating children's books. Since then she has created many books, mostly in her highly successful and entertaining comic-strip style. Although some of her books, like *My Secret War Diary by Flossie Albright* and *Lizzy Bennet's Diary,* have edged across the border towards novels, this is her first book written entirely in that form. Marcia lives in a dog kennel, which she shares with one hairy saint and one hairy sinner.

1.

1. Marcia Williams (left) and Olga Henderson (neé Morris) visiting the Imperial War Museum (where the Changi quilt is now kept), London 2017.

2. A section from the Changi quilt, by Olga Morris.

3. Olga Morris as a child in Singapore.

3.

2.

© Imperial War Museum (EPH 9206, cropped)